THE LEGEND OF HENRY McCOOL
Book One

I0555622

"Mike Cloud Devine is not only at play in the fields of the Grand Lexicon, he is at home there, creating magical images of the chaos of pastoral man trying to survive in the Frankensteinian world of techno-overkill. Henry leads us through his loose Lovingtown asylum world like Tireseus leading the blinded seekers of bottom-line 21st century life. I have read Mr. Devine's manuscript four times. The only other book I have read through and through more than three times is James Joyce's *Ulysses*. Devine's story deserves at least one reading, after which I am sure you, as did I, will want more."

—JOHN G. NELSON

ALSO BY MIKE CLOUD DEVINE

The Legend of Henry McCool–Book Two
Ts'ai Lun Press

Lost Highway (CD)
Mike Cloud Devine Music

Festival of Depression (CD)
Mike Cloud Devine Music

The LEGEND of HENRY McCOOL

Book One

a novel by

MIKE CLOUD DEVINE

TS'AI LUN PRESS

© 2025 by Mike Cloud Devine
All Rights Reserved.

No part of this book may be reproduced or transmitted
in any form or by any means, graphic, electronic, or
mechanical, including photocopying, recording, taping or
by any information storage or retrieval system, without
the written permission of the publisher, except for brief
passages used in a review.

This is a work of fiction. Names, characters, places, and
incidents are the product of the author's imagination
or are used fictitiously for the edification of posterity,
and any resemblance to actual persons, living or dead,
business establishments, events, or locales is entirely
coincidental.

Library of Congress Cataloging-in-Publication Data

Devine, Mike Cloud, author.
The Legend of Henry McCool—Book One /
by Mike Cloud Devine.

ISBN: 979-8-9993722-1-5 (paperback)
Library of Congress Control Number: 2025914184

1. Fiction 2. Magical realism

Ts'ai Lun Press
West Front Street, Box 7
Livingston MT 59047
tsailunpress.com

Book design by Kathleen Dexter – KDInkandImage.net

No AI was used in the creation of this book.

ACKNOWLEDGEMENTS

Books One and Two
The Legend of Henry McCool

The writing of this novel has been a decades-long juggernaut of discovery. I would not have completed it without the generosity of those along the way, the help and encouragement of friends, and the love and support of my family.

After the big idea for the novel had come to me I scratched around for a story and characters. By serendipitous happenstance the *Mainstreet Show* was born. In desperate times for a town, creative smart people lent themselves to the distraction of a stage.

The novel's characters and storyline, including Henry McCool, Sugarfoot, and friends, build on an ongoing series of monologues featured as part of the *Mainstreet Show*. Throughout my time at the helm of the show Henry's stories and wild adventures shared the stage, radio, and television with writers such as Greg Keeler, William Hjortsberg, Tim Cahill, Henry Real Bird, and many others. Performing over the near thirty-year run of the show with numerous artists such as Jeff Bridges, Margot Kidder, Bill Payne, Kostas, Deb Corbett, The Irrigators, Sean Devine, and Rich Hall kept the bar high for developing *The Legend of Henry McCool* and his music. To those named and unnamed, I am deeply grateful and indebted for their association.

I would like to acknowledge trauma for strengthening my determination to give up any aspirations for the comfy life in order to travel at street level, which allowed me to concentrate my efforts on exploring for a vehicle to express my thoughts. I want to acknowledge poverty as the only answer I had for gaining the time necessary to devote to this work. Neighbors wondered—nobody knows what he does.

I want to acknowledge the beds and weight benches I have taken advantage of—the important hours of no-questions-asked relief. I also want to thank the supine position that has always been a cradle of creativity when I need daydreaming. There are the bedside chairs and leather folder to be thankful for for quietly accommodating my inspirations at any hour anywhere I happen to be.

Special thanks to Maryanne Vollers, Marian Hjortsberg, and Andrea Peacock for their comments as the story progressed; to Hannibal Anderson for countless sessions airing it out; to Kumiko O, Kobe, for calligraphy; to René Aftring and Doris Löffler for handing me West Berlin.

Special thanks to Sean Evers, Brendan Hearty, Pat Neary, Shay and Padraig at Macnas, in Galway; the Rynne family for Downings House library, Kildare; Henry McCullough, Coleraine; Kathi B, Alex, Anya, and Gudrun, in Berlin, for their muse and critique.

Special thanks to Dorothy Bradley and to Tom Brokaw for giving me the nod to test the waters with a theatrical announcement of a candidacy for the Perusiduncy of the Untidy Status of Eureka at Dorothy's campaign stop on the West Boulder River.

Very special thanks to Diane Smith who encouraged me early and remained unwavering through the years of development with her wisdom and professional direction; Barney Hallin for literally holding down the fort in Montana for this fiction-in-the-time-of-Covid to take shape; my sidekick

Greg Keeler who is always inspiring with his own brand of genius input, comedic and otherwise; Merlita Mojares who contributed mightily to stabilizing the unpredictable situation of care giving, helping me to bring this story to fruition; Gordon 'Corky' Brittan whose validating insights came generously and with perfect timing. Special thanks to Kathleen Dexter for her comma wrangling and for coming on to clean things up and shepherd the book through the publishing processes with her steady maven's hand.

To those mentioned, and with apologies for those unmentioned (there is no good place to stop), I extend my sincere gratitude for making this a better story. I am solely responsible for any errors or omissions.

And, as important as any, a loving thanks to all those authors, dead and living, who took the time to write down every word I've read—Where would I be without you?!

For everyone who reads

Henry has clear memories from the age of five of trying to get his head wholly around the trinity. He was telling me the Sisters of Mercy tried the trinity out on him and he did not know if it was himself or them but there was bound to be a misunderstanding and it was uncomfortable. I am only five, he remembers begging the sisters, I'm trying.

That's when Henry went home and drilled out the croquet mallet. He unscrewed the long handle of the croquet mallet and drilled in from one end of the head. He proceeded to scale the block wall in the backyard, tamp tobacco in the handle hole of the mallet head, put a Lucifer to it and inhale his first. It did not help. Smoking the croquet mallet did not help, said Henry, but the coughing and thinking put his mind at ease.

Not long after the croquet mallet incident Henry's family moved to the edge of town. As it seemed unlikely that Henry could be persuaded into any fold, his parents hoped he might do better in a place with a little more room to explore his nature.

It did feel pretty good in fresh country. Henry walked Strawberry Trail to the Little League Fields for ball-throw practice smoking from his first pack of Chesterfields. The late afternoon sun through the trees was a silent festival of light and shadow and gave the ground he so concentrated on a kind of serendipitous, poetic feel. His new friend Johnny Bill Rose lived on Dapplegray Lane. Henry said he had just gone by Dapplegray Lane thinking of the words moving along like they do—Johnny Bill Rose on Dapplegray Lane. All he wanted to do, promised Henry, was to expand this nice picture in his mind when it happened again. Dapplegray Lane is off Palos Verde Drive North. Seems like you should be going north on Palos Verde Drive North, thought Henry, but you don't go north on Palos Verde Drive North. You go east or west on Palos Verde Drive North. You can't go north on Palos Verde Drive North.

Why do they do that? Henry asked himself. Why doesn't someone do something about it?

Henry's whole world went south over Palos Verde Drive North. He kicked around at ball throw for a few years but it was clear another strategy was needed.

Henry said his father was a sailor. He told Henry at the age of eight or nine that he could tell by the cut of his jib that Henry's sails were set for an uncommon destiny.

Henry said he remembers being in his room at a folding card table one Sunday after church. He was building a free-flight gas craft out of doped silk and balsa when he heard his father tell his mother to come out to the car. He had something in the car to show her. Though barely a whisper, the sound of his father's voice cocked Henry's head to one side. His father had just cracked open the door to Henry's room, looked around with a smile and closed the door without a word. Henry said the suspicious air made him take up a position in his lilac blind to overhear his parents talking about the outcome of a meeting with a state social worker.

It seemed the social worker had taken Henry's case to committee and advice had come back to get in touch with the Federal Seeing Eye Agency about filling an opening in the Agency's control experiment for an asylum on the moon. The committee's recommendation, it turned out, was gospel.

Henry said his parents sat him down at Sunday supper to inform him of a promising opportunity that had come his way: there was an opening for Henry in Lovingtown, Montana, not far from a national park.

Henry said when he arrived the Agency representative received him with a disconcerting eager pleasure. She was sure Henry would find Lovingtown a friendly place with plenty of room to roam. He was told the trick to being happy in Lovingtown was to become goal oriented. The goal is to get out as often as you can, but remember, she pointed out, you will come back because emotionally and psychologically you are committed to the area.

You get institutionalized, said Henry, adjusting himself to go on at some length with the interview. You know you can't stay away so you have another patient water the plants and pay the bills until you return.

In the asylum everyone is patient for the wind to die down. We stay patient here in town (as we like to call it) and take our medicines. We are not supposed to drink with our medications but we do exercise before we go to Happy Hour. As a matter of fact, patented Henry, Happy Hour is when all the exercises start to make you feel better. You begin to feel like a gentle swell in a pool and then as your lids hang low you imagine yourself one of the rich swells at poolside.

There are no rich people in the asylum, Henry offered, because they can afford to stay home and bring help in. However, there are rich people claiming the place for an address, marooning themselves in a huge pasture like they are on the high seas in amber waves or tucking into some high country hideaway like the asylum can't see them.

In town, Henry generalized, we try to make the rich feel comfortable ... not pried upon, and what do they do? They go and buy automobiles you cannot pay for with a job in the asylum—you can't help but notice them. You can tell them they can get to town a lot cheaper than that but they will not listen. They have seen themselves in the very car on television.

Henry says he sees them in their television cars going through town, but you do not see them stop in town. Henry understands the television cars are cruising through on their way to Bidnith, as usual. He says he has heard that purchase power is nosegay in the city of Bidnith.

Bidnith is supposed to be a real nice place. We are like twin towns I have heard, said Henry, not like identical twins but more like bi-polar twins. And there *are* opposing qualities but it is hard to believe the wind does not blow badly in Bidnith like they say; and to believe the people of Bidnith do not drink with their medications ... well I don't know, doubts Henry, that invites incredulity.

Bidnith is right around here somewhere. Inmates swear it is not that far from the asylum. Henry says he hasn't found Bidnith yet but it must be on the map. I know Bidnith is on the map, he says, because when you see the swells in the big four-wheel drives with the windows rolled up and looking air-conditioned fresh, you can tell they must be from someplace on the map. I will find it someday, Henry pledged, but *getting down to Bidnith* as they say, is not really a clue to where it is located. Down to Henry is down river, but to some people down is south and from the asylum these are two different directions. Down river is one way and south of asylum is another.

I am pretty sure of a couple of things, Henry consoled himself. I know it must be paved all the way to Bidnith because the cars and trucks and Humvees are clean. I expect Bidnith is pretty well manicured too, because the people are said to be talking all the time about taking care of it.

No matter how hard one tries to make it okay, the rich consider themselves anomalies in Lovingtown, Henry went on without prompting, and they feel uncomfortable, so they go to Bidnith to shop where they can be an anomaly in anonymity. And by god, Henry shucked playacting, I hear tell when you get all the anomalies together down'n Bidnith ... damned if they don't all look alike. They say if you go looking for someone in Bidnith you think you see them everywhere and a lot of innocent people are accosted.

Shouldn't something be done about it?

Did I never tell the trouble I had getting down to Bidnith? Henry extended the dramatics. Trouble toured when my beret was blown off and tread upon. Scars on me too, he pointed.

One morning early I thought I would get down to Bidnith just to have a look, said Henry, so I asked a local longtimer what he thought. Longtimer said he had not been out enough to get to Bidnith himself but he heard tell you would recognize Bidnith when you got there by the three houses and cemetery that surround a city on a hill. You can see the father's house, he says, up on top of the hill and down below it a ways there is the son's house and about two-thirds up from the son's to the father's you take a left for a shorter ways to the ghost house. Henry nodded. Longtimer answered the nod and carried on. Nobody will live in the ghost house. You see, Bidnith is not without its problems, Longtimer said parenthetically. Now you go back down the road from the ghost house, cross the intersection and go the same shorter ways and you are at the cemetery. The cemetery is in the Paydirt Subdivision: all small farms. I understand the intersection of the cross streets is the heart of Bidnith. You come to a town laid out like I am telling you and mister you are in Bidnith, Longtimer guaranteed.

Just a few words about the problems in Bidnith, cautioned Longtimer, besides the ghost house, part of the problem in Bidnith is the cemetery. You see, Longtimer went with hearsay, Bidnith is an age with grace, die with dignity kind of place following the Slamdammit Mondaymentalist traditions—neat and tidy like. The people of Bidnith are smiley and dressed fashionably nice in their outward casualness but you have to understand that everything—every little thing—is kept real close track of in Bidnith. That is the real spooking thing about Bidnith. In Bidnith, besides the ghost house problem, there is one remains missing at the cemetery and one extra person in town and they cannot seem to figure out who's who or what's what so they go off like a bunch of berserkers at play in some kind of epiphanical chaos. It does seem something should be done about it.

CHAPTER TWO

Digesting what Longtimer had told him, Henry said he was reminded he had put off grocery shopping beyond the point. It was a down-to-canned-vegetables-and-pickles-in-the-pantry situation, he explained.

Most important at a moment like this, Henry said, is waiting for a window of opportunity in one's psychological condition agreeable to grocery shopping. Timing is everything. The consequences of who you will meet at the grocery store or what might happen on the way weigh-in heavily on Henry. A trip to the market, he justified, may forever alter your future. The truth is, said Henry, if he had not picked up clues to the whatabouts of Bidnith from Longtimer he may not yet have mustered the motivation to shop. He would need good nutrition on an expedition to Bidnith.

Psychological progress, if made at all, is measured in ever-so-teensy increments, Henry magnified.

Henry keeps a shopping list, writing down things as he runs out of them. It is part of the household ceremony, he says. Henry knows he could save any one of the lists to use over and over because the lists are always the same but he says he likes the commiseration with the cupboards losing, the list gaining, teetering with the shifting burden from pantry to paper—the list lengthens, the cupboards bare—until shopping day when the teeter totters back to the cupboards under the weight of the fresh food stuffs. It does not matter that the process of list making ensures Henry buys the same things over and over because the list is new. A fresh list may be one of those teensy increments, Henry cautioned; you just never know.

There is a resignation with the futile in the household futilities of wash dish laundry list, Henry spilled forth. He feels that woman's near acquaintance with domestic futilities is responsible for her distinguishing behavioral characteristics. Henry says he could shop without a list but the list will not let him down.

The list Henry pulled from the clip on the frig this late morning contained a special addition against a day's journey: trail mix to go with the flow on an exploration for Bidnith. Henry planned for one whole day away from the asylum but brought medications along as preparations for the unexpected. For the trip to Bidnith he also carried a trinity of tools in a black leather satchel: a flashlight for the ghost house; an archaeologist's trowel for the missing remains; and a teensy tiny wrist watch camera for recording and counting the people of Bidnith in hopes of solving their mystery.

Henry left home to greet the glorious extravagance of an unseasonably warm winter morning, which caused a pause of shock, relief, and joy to pass through him in a delightful crescendo of emotion. He hopped into the fuzztop and made streak for the store.

Henry wheeled his cart into the fruits where his eyes finished their roving at the sight of a lovely woman of foreign descriptions. Something feral goes on, Henry confessed, when a woman's mind is distant in appreciation of clutch-and-release at the banana bin. Henry's interest piqued.

The answer to my transfixion came, he said, the instant her bumbling limbs froze for the rotating look of astonishment as she answered her shopmate with a question:

Why would anyone want to buy green bananas? she asked.

Henry knew this one was not from the asylum.

Because they last longer, the shopmate answered.

Henry knew shopmate was from the asylum. Green bananas give the asylum a sense of the future.

Henry imposed on the shoppers to ask where the foreigner was from, the impact of the inquiry explaining itself on the changing contours of her face.

What business is it of yours? she answered—not rude but inquisitive and playfully dramatic.

Oh, nothing. Sorry to startle, Henry apologized, bowing out and moving off to his own big bin, thinking to himself that her answer was signal enough. She may be the one to lead him to Bidnith. He had to abandon his shopping, he said adding, one must lock into the timing. You feel the timing ... you don't control it, he surrendered. What one must do must be done.

Henry tailed the shoppers through checkout to parking lot and disappointment. The foreign object of his desire was not driving a television car. She must be on visitation to the asylum, Henry slumped. She would be no help leading him to Bidnith. Henry spent part of the afternoon in the car in the parking lot pondering what could have been when he noticed the keys in the ignition and the thought came to him to drive. Henry said he had not driven south much of a distance when a cerebral stimulation of the synaptic kind notified his cognizance of a shortage of batteries for flashlighting. Better late synapse than never, Henry rejoiced, recounting the score and three-quarters since his first encounter with a stranger stimulating his nervous system.

Henry angled off the highway into an old-west strip mall for the purpose of battery procurement and pulled in front of a proper façade. He opened the car door, moving to get out and reaching back for the flashlight on the front seat at the same time. The wind promptly smashed the door into his shins provoking a summoning of the Almighty to pass immediate judgment. The simultaneous physical reaction to attend the wounded site produced a hammering of Henry's head on the headliner, jarring loose his beret, enabling its capture by the wind. A gust gorged the crown, wheeling the beret across the gravel at an impossible angle to the ground, Henry observed, at a most improbable speed, reminiscent of Frisbee failure, he analyzed.

The beret took aim at a fine gentleman of potato proportions distracted by Henry's loud oath from his project of loading a giant screen TV into a formidable television truck. In an Olympian display of timing and agility Potatoman poised and pounced; treading on the beret, ending its expedition in a grave of gravel.

Henry was not far behind the beret and reaching Potatoman (posed like a peacock in triumphant pride) their eyes met, the vision of an icon of disgust masterly sculpted for Potatoman's countenance, and TV—the daily destination— the cause of his distraction. Henry ciphered the sound-bitten eyes. His attention was drawn by bleary whites, glazed irises, and beady pupils to a perforated mind where all but bleak thought had been banished: mob boss, charred body, Dow down, soldier charged, storm kills, under pressure, tourist injured, new jail, settlers go, women tell, men die, those killed, addicted mothers, state sues, record lottery, bad fats, suicide, offshore, fairer press, hit home, ED, speed kills, whatever you need, win big, plane crash, sprawl film, drug summit, final days, twelve months, no interest, close out, lose weight, rich/ poor gap grows, guilty, poison, fine print, late tax, default, paralyzed, death comes, toxic waste, minute free, foul play, can't prove, spur decision, Russia vows, get connected, tough truck, rivals square off.

Nice stop! Henry congratulated, bending to rob the grave. He returned to the potato face to notice it hanging heavily before thieving a glance at the big man's watch. If I go back soon, Henry computed in the privacy of his mind, I will make it in time for one at Happy Hour. Thank you, sir. I was wondering, said Henry, wanting to go on with a short query of Potatoman's knowledge of Bidnith when he sensed a snap in spudman's spam of attention and wondered what, if anything, could be done about it.

CHAPTER THREE

Having rescued his beret Henry said he bowed out gracefully from under the snap in spudman's spam of attention and went inside an old west strip-mall store to pick up flashlight batteries even though he had nearly decided to give up Bidnith concerns for the day and head back in for one during Happy Hour at the Bar'n Grille.

Henry said he had scolded himself to promise to recover his grocery shopping volition after Happy Hour but a thought to visit the river overcame him and the thought was not resistible. The day had managed to stay mild into the evening and the moon, accompanied by an entourage of wispy clouds, was a full half. It was a beautiful evening for a drive on the river, he said to himself, and he knew just where to go.

A river runs through the asylum and Henry decided to *shortcut* through a special glaze to a rendezvous with riprap. Henry said he knows *shortcut* sounds complicated but it is really simple. At the Bar'n Grille a picture frame encloses a special kind of window to a special kind of riprap. It is not the only window of its kind. You see, Henry leaned in, there are windows all around the Bar'n Grille, some windows look to the sidewalks and streets right outside and others look out on scenes farther away. Some look out on the Elk River and grass and trees and mountains and sky. The owner of the Bar'n Grille put shades on the windows to the street but he put a special glaze on the picture-framed *windows* to the interiors of the asylum. The special glaze is meant to subdue bright colors trying to get through the pane because bright colors tend to react with patient's medications and the Bar'n Grille is where the asylum sips.

To illustrate his point Henry related that he was once in deep conversation with a four-year-old asylum dweller when she confided in him that a particular green made her eat her necklace ... especially when the sun came out.

The special glaze creates a landscape in a minor key much like great composers write when sanity escapes them and they feel a possible pass to the Great Perhaps.

Henry said he arrived at the Bar'n Grille, slung on his black leather satchel of tools from the fuzztop front seat, took a stool at the bar, and played everything like normal: a drink or two with greetings all around, disguising his intentions to *shortcut*. He kept his eye on the special glaze he would leave through and waited for the table below to be vacated. Leaving the asylum through a special glaze, Henry whispered, is on the QT. Even though the rules around Lovingtown are loose the Agency looks upon it as intent-to-escape.

Henry took the table under the special glaze that looked out to a spot on the Elk he knows well: the evening's destination. Henry said he always spends a little time at the table beneath the special glaze listening to the minor key composition for guards rustling in the trees. Guards are hiding in the trees of the landscape to guide people back to the asylum when they would otherwise wander away. Listening to see guards in the landscape is no problem for the inmates, Henry admits; you have to be able to stare for a long time—that is the secret. You could make it more difficult for guards by wearing camouflage but in the Bar'n Grille camouflage is conspicuous, he cautioned. Also, there is no TV in the Bar'n Grille to distract inmates with commercials now and then interrupted by programming, so you have to be a patient patient for the timing to slip out, he instructed.

That night the scenario looked good. It was not a problem giving the inmates the slip. The guards were on the far side of the moat-like river and Henry's destination was on the near side. It is not a big deal if you get caught but it can spoil an outing.

Once you are out, Henry warned, the tricky part is finding the exact spot where you can get back in by *shortcut*. Otherwise it could be a long walk back to your place. You can do the Hansel and Gretel thing, he acknowledged, but Sacagawea's geese are trained to collect the droppings and alert the guards (the messiah ward in the asylum is full of those unfortunates who went into the forest and had their bread crumbs eaten). There is a park in the asylum named for Sacagawea and famous for droppings but that is another story altogether, said Henry. Anyway, when you hear geese honking hard flying low you know someone is getting caught shortcutting.

Henry said he made his move and slipped through the picture-framed glaze. If you are wondering what it is like, said Henry aside, there is no sensation to it; you shrink into perspective like you always do.

It was actually a short trip through the foreground grass with no guards or geese to contend with, he said, and it was no time till he arrived at the carbody riprap for the late evening drive along the river.

The carbody is perfectly placed. This time of year it is dry and at water level, half buried in the bank, steering wheel and driver's-side seat springs exposed. There is no roof on the car but the driver's-side door is closed, without glass and partly sunken subterranean. Henry checked out the interior of his ride with flashlight, leaned in the door window, and made the seat a little wider with the archaeologist's trowel.

He climbed over dash and door, took the driver's seat, and started the engine. While the motor was warming up Henry said he propped the flashlight on the dash between two willows like an askew headlamp shining out across the water, the reflections off the on-coming current frolicking towards him through the cinemascaped night.

The car is perfectly placed because you have the driver's side headed up stream and next to the water. The drive does not work the same going down river, explained Henry, because you have to do the Einstein thing and work with relativity in order to make the drive come together. You close down your field of vision to the flashlit water out the door's window frame and then ... magic: you move and the water stills. It is no longer a scene of a river going by a carbody stuck in a dirt bank with some nut-case sitting in there pretending a drive; it is an evening for touring.

Henry put the car in gear and took off on a drive up Elk River. The wispy clouds from the south moving across the face of the moon helped drop Henry headlong into the illusion ... or was it reality? he equiponderated. Henry said he was clipping right along through the big artist's delicate design making time by the light of the moon with a headlamp shining out across the current, feeling like a king with a carload of concubines in constant attention against the pang of desire when he was suddenly struck broadside by aloneness. The spell had broken. The car stopped and the river flowed. As he wondered what happened to the drive

Henry said he remembered Valentine's Day was on Monday coming so he got out pen and paper and wrote a Valentine's Day letter to the moon to appease her should her feelings have been hurt:

Dear Moon, I finished painting a portrait of you yesterday. It is oil-on-canvas. It is my most favorite painting I have ever done. I was so nervous to get started on the painting because you are so important to me but once I got started painting I could hardly stop to rest from working on it. My friends would visit me but I would keep working. They would watch and talk and sometimes I would not hear them and forget they were there. My friends say the portrait looks just like you. I hope you will like it. The painting is drying on an easel on the big table by the grist mill. Today is Friday. This coming Monday is a holiday. It is Valentine's Day. Do you know Valentine's Day? It is a special day for the person you love and I write this letter to you, Moon, for Valentine's Day because you are the one I love. You are the person I am waiting for. Waiting for the person you love can make anything seem like a very long time. I really want to be with you but writing and painting is the best I can do right now and right now I just want to sit here and write to tell you how much you are wanted and needed and loved. And so I write: Dearest Moon, I love you. Will you be my Valentine?

Henry said he signed, and the moon listened and read and suffered no verbal incontinence. Henry swooned; she is the mother of all earth's dumbnation.

CHAPTER FOUR

Still sitting in the carbody riprap Henry looked over his Valentine's ode to the moon one more time, being in company with her like he was. He paused at the end of his missive waiting for an audible response, seductively stealing another glance at her. Wispy clouds were scattered around her here and there like angels around a dead planet. Henry countered the death idea by reintroducing himself to the moon:

Good evening, I am Henry. I believe you to be a lovely lady and I'm enamored of your charms, he said out loud. It was the *I am Henry* that hollowed his mind. He said he thought of himself, this person, this me, this corpus called Henry: a being, a thing by a name, how small. He said his own name sounded estranged. Disassociated he said was his thinking, leaning his head back, pressing his torso into the squealing springs, imagining their circular orbits of rust printed like targets on the back of his jacket and wondering if he was dead before he was born, of lost memory of manly spermhood, the swim and fight, the female-centric ovum tumbling down and the first encounter, the give and take to get along. These are your roots of disorder and every other earthly problem, he said triumphantly, congratulating himself with a burst of force from his legs, sending his back into the targets under a steady pressure for another look at the moon and her graveyard friends.

At the frayed ends of thought Henry said he mulled over the ragged edges of the torn clouds looking like feathers of an angel. He said he closed his eyes so he could see more clearly—Oh yes, heaven is a flying dream. Hell is a nightmare. Die in your sleep in the middle of a good dream, thought Henry, and the dream is eternal heaven. You should be damned happy to wake from a bad dream, he deduced.

Henry said heaven is a nice idea but, just in case, he wants to be freshly ground and fed to a 4-H hog raised by relatives for their Easter Sunday supper, recycling the best part of him back into the bosom of the family, double-filtered pure. Extract of Henry. Henry concentrate.

And so he did. Arousing himself from the aura Henry gripped the flashlight between the willows, removed it from the dash and climbed out and up onto the carbody, seat springs giving up the right foot with a snap and rattle in a cloud of rust dust. He paused standing on the dash and front quarter panel sweeping the river's edge with flashlight, looking for ankle twisters, deciding whether to jump or climb, when he noticed fishing wader tracks in the light: semi-spherical cleats of strategically placed bumps on the bottom of a boot. Seeing his way clear, Henry jumped to the firm sand of the river's edge for closer reconnaissance, laughing to himself at a fisherman worried about the size of his fish. Fishermen always worry the size of their fish. Casting their big fish story, Henry thought. But to the listener, allowing for fisherman to count some of the water the fish was swimming out of and some of the water the fish was swimming into, the fish was really more like a little less big.

Henry followed the wader tracks leaving the carbody riprap in the bank of the river behind. The wader tracks led to a sandy beach at the edge of a deep hole carved by eddying water. The bumps on the boots had churned the sand into a site of consolidated disturbance. Wonder how fisherman did here? Henry asked himself. How big was his fish? Henry had a closing laugh and turned to leave the fishing hole when he noticed at the transition zone of willows and sand an odd piece of debris reflecting the glow of the flashlight. He said he hunkered down on his haunches for a closer examination. Oh yes, Henry remarked with embarrassing familiarity, a turn-of-the-millennium artifact in a landfill-lover's paradise: the condom. His belly bubbled from a chuckle at the New Age litter before quite unexpectedly noticing the bumps on the prophylactic matching in miniature the traction bumps on the bottom of the boots. He mused to himself how these little nineties icons are seen regularly scattered about these days like sea shells in sand, and wondered what it would sound like if you held one up to your ear? For that matter, Henry deliberated, trying to preserve a tinge of the proper while indulging the absurd, what would one hear if one were to hold waders up to one's ear? Never mind. He was put off the thought immediately. However, Henry then reconciled, posturing himself in earnest, right forefinger conducting his lips, with the proverbial leaky seam in one's waders the sounds sealed in waders and condom may not be all that different, maybe a little matter of emphasis, he noted analytically. Henry said he played archaeologist and troweled the treasure deep in a sandy grave, snapped a shot, but planned no cryptic cartography.

Leaving the scene of landfill love Henry said he came to a bank of stratified garbage that could take you back decades if not centuries to tetanus. That is another story, Henry stifled himself, knowing he needed to get on the trail of the *shortcut* back to the Bar'n Grille. But not before congratulating himself once again, however, that thanks to him, Henry, not all garbage is in landfill because part of it is home. Henry says he has a collection of containers he has not the will to part with ... to let go of ... to throw away. If he ever needed anything like this container this container would be perfect. If I ever need a jug with a ring handle around its neck this jug will be perfect, Henry defended. This thought managed to remind Henry to get the grocery shopping done. Shop groceries shop groceries, he drilled.

Henry wended his way through willows up the landfill bank out of the river bottom and into the foreground grass, noting his passing thought of the Landfill Bank of Lovingtown as evidence in favor of complex neurological associations.

Looking back and ahead, again and again, lining himself up survey sure with the scene he saw out the special glaze at the Bar'n Grille Henry walked towards *shortcut* reentry. It can be tricky. You will not see light until you are looking in the window at fog-up distance. As you approach the pane from the outside you listen closely for the ringing of rumor's bells like muted chimes in the same minor key you left leaving. The wind came up Henry's back, he said, making it difficult to hold his course, and more troublesome for hearing the subtle sounds of ancient chimes coming from inside the Bar'n Grille. Henry slowed his pace for fear of going past the pane and kept looking, checking his alignment behind him. There is some recourse to instrument navigation, said Henry, kind of an asylum autopilot—an inmate's omni. You see, Henry took me in confidence, since you are not at the Bar'n Grille they will most probably be talking about you ... you are lucky, it makes it easier. Your ears will heat up. The hotter your ears get the closer you are to the pane.

Henry's ears warmed. He began traversing an invisible plane back and forth, ears cooling, warming, locking in on a path of increasing heat. Sounds coming. Chimes calling. He said he heard a familiar voice say: He was here earlier but then he just disappeared, vanished. Henry stood at the window and looked in. Not a big hubbub, he judged. He looked back for a last glance at his Valentine, picked his time, and slipped inside gracefully to notice he hadn't been seen. In no time, though, an asylum sister saw Henry and came over to him.

Oh there you are! You were here earlier weren't you? I didn't see you leave. We were just talking about you. I didn't see you come in either! Where were you?

Ah, nowhere.

What have you been doing?

Nothing really, same old stuff, nothing ever changes, he concluded.

The asylum sister returned to her crowd to retrieve her drink but the hubbub began to close in on Henry.

Did you see on television where ... you see the sunset ... mud's a bad sign ... I'm not going to let him do that to me! ... the republicans are ... forty-seven stitches along my ... If I were president ... Wall Street ... The cacophony was a *go-sign* Henry heeded.

Chapter Five

Henry stalled in the scene at the Bar'n Grille re-summoning the psychology to shop, he said, and went over an outline of activities for his next couple hours: go home, get mail, feed dog, and get groceries ... prioritized. He decided to stay and have one for the store because the women at the Bar'n Grille were grouping for a passion project and he got interested to know. It turned out, said Henry, that it was a pre-meeting for a fundraiser and after he suggested the group have a women's smoker to raise funds for battered women's *Project Relax* he said he got stunk so bad he was lucky to get down from the cross and make it home at all.

Henry said he finished his drink and with a hurried goodbye took the fuzztop home to a celebrated welcome by Franklin. Franklin is Henry's dog. Henry says the diamond in Franklin's half-shepherd half-husky crown is that he does all his barking in his dreams. Both went inside the shack. Henry fed Franklin and fumbled for the grocery list. The list Franklin, where is the list? Oh god! Where is the list? An incident like this can cost Henry a couple days in bed, he admitted. He would rather not.

One of the adjustments of winter is having the many pockets of laundry to look through and nothing is more devastating to Henry than to lose something on his own person. You scratch around like you are covered with lice, said Henry, and you never know if the loss will be found. It is better to be burnt at the stake, he edified. It must have fallen out at the river when I took the paper out of my pocket to write the ode to the moon, he thought while he searched pants, shirt, vest, jacket, and overcoat. Outside pockets, inside pockets, front to back, back to front, top to bottom, bottom to top. Henry said time fueled the frenetics to a nutcase frenzy as he searched for thing lost. In the frenzy he said he imagined the object lying peacefully somewhere outside his domain: a list lying on the sandy floorboard of an old carbody; a simple paper resting beside willows coming up through a transmission. God can see it! Heaven knows right where the damned thing is, Henry taunted, and a great time was had by all with a frisk routine on a one-man cop show at Henry's expense, he grieved.

In the presence of heaven the dog was bored by Henry's buffoonery and lay his belly down and stretched his neck to rest his chin on the floor, well settled for a long wait, when Henry half shouted from momentary clarity:

Get in the car, Franklin; we're shopping without a list.

Henry said the two of them loaded up in the fuzztop and went to market. There were no significant incidents on the way and Franklin was on guard in the unlocked car when Henry went through the automatic doors and into the melee. Not that there were a lot of people shopping. There were not. But the loss of the list meant Henry had to shop by prompter: he can remember what was on the list if he sees it on a shelf, and sadly, that means taking all the aisles. It is traumatic for Henry because each item in the store comes complete with history and future and it is not always pretty.

Henry assumes most people prefer a good hoodwinking or there would be more people in the asylum. Most people do not care about where chickens or cows or chemicals come from, he ventured. They must prefer to put faith in the Landfill Bank of Lovingtown and pretend money is not the bottom layer. Not a lot different from Franklin, Henry thought: dog food comes in a dish. That's that. Amen.

Once inside the store, Henry said he made his way past a million magazines and a thousand shapes of sugar to come to eggs and cracked right into the terror of it all. Go ahead, Henry prodded, ask someone which came first the chicken or the egg and they will never again wonder about another thing in their life. Chicken farms? I don't know. Slaughterhouses? May be. No, from then on it is the egg tree, the chicken tree, the steak tree, the sugar tree, and the snack-food tree.

Henry said he wants to point out that the which-came-first-the-chicken-or-the-egg question is like asking which came first the horse and donkey or the mule. Henry would ask for special attention to this important matter but he is fully aware that consequences make a life, and he is really afraid of the reaction to this point and the subsequent consequences for his psychological condition. Consequences of this magnitude can put Henry to bed for weeks, he admitted again, where he reads great literature of thingsneverchange.

The history of every item in the store is only the half of it, Henry exclaimed, the future is another thing altogether. It is a terrible tragedy of realism that you must mix earth and water and air together in different proportions to get everything: everything from tractor to turnip. And forget pure ingredients, Henry mea culpaed, plain clean ingredients are hard to come by.

The grocery store is only a spoke in the wheel of the cycle of warehousing waste, Henry waxed poetic. On the shelf one day, in the landfill, into the air, treatment plant to the river the next. And one *HAS* to shop, Henry emphasized half disturbed. Beads of sweat on his forehead and worry in his eyes made me wonder the worth of continuing the story without taking a break when he wailed about the wine shelves and remembered to me the last time through how he carefully counted the twelve steps it took to get from one end of the wine aisle to the other and spewed out he cut down his drinking. Just ask the garbage man, Henry said; the garbage man knows who does what.

But even sober, Henry tuned up, you are going to come to the aisle of organic foods and natural foods and health foods and have to wonder what is in the rest of the store.

Leaning on his cart, Henry said he speculated on a short sketch of shopper psychology: get the heart rate up with magazines and sugar, sell them the egg story, run them through the wine, and hit them with the chemicals ... tub cleaners, oven cleaners, toilet cleaners, cleaner cleaners, paper masks, rubber gloves, plastic brushes ... and hope by the time they get through the impulse racks to the fresh meat, vegetables, and fruit on the perimeter of the store they shall be numbed to exhaustion from the gauntlet and shalt not wonder if chemicals ever get into food.

They have survived beer cases under ham counter, popcorn at videos, deodorant by pasta, toothpaste by tuna, cough drops by sardines and a sleight-of-mind drop into institutional foods: Kool Aid, Power Aid (the lures); body refreshers (the rewards); halogen bulbs with plastic dinnerware (the interrogation); is it a mirror or are you twisting like the pretzel on the counter before you? (the confusion); easy cheese and crackers (you are succumbing); razor blades and Cocoa Pebbles (draw the bath water); soft white light bulbs and Chips Ahoy! It is a small wonder there are not more suicides at the grocery store, Henry said wearily. You would think something would be done about it.

Henry said he finally made it back to the banana bin for something to go with cottage cheese. He recalled the foreign girl failure from the stifled shop earlier in the day as he coerced his cart toward the check-out counter with the right front wheel fluttering like a dying fly on its back on the sill while he put cotton in his ears and applied an alcohol-soaked handkerchief to his forehead for the final assault through chewing gum and carcass photos, where the last thing he remembered before he collapsed in the cart was someone asking if he preferred paper or plastic.

Henry said he was only down a little while when he was aroused by the scent of a woman and came to consciousness assisted by a beautiful girl of dark hair and dark eyes and soft warm-colored skin, the unexpected visitation of an angel returned by god to the asylum from a college of forensic psychology. Henry said he was embarrassed of his condition but pleased to see her. She asked if he was going to be all right and Henry said he nodded yes.

You are looking beautiful!

So are you, she said. I've got to run. Let's get together, she added.

Goodbye, said Henry. Thank you. We will be in touch.

Her walk away required him to notice she was in the sensual shape of the recently singled and, said Henry, hope rose through unforeseeable circumstances like a beam of light through sunburned fog shining down on the lost and forgotten of limbo.

CHAPTER SIX

Henry said he collected himself at the check-out counter, shaking off the trauma of the shopping gauntlet, and sifted through thoughts of the woman to his rescue. The bagging and beeping at checkout, however, sustained him in his puzzledom and prevented him appearing present and accounted for. Check writing competed with biblical tomes for length and creativity. Henry said the last time he asked the clerk for the date and the amount she asked him for a photo ID sensing it would be a polite reminder to him of who he was and where to go next with the groceries.

Henry loaded plastic bags of food into the trunk of the fuzztop, carefully placing the sacks around the migrating spare tire, and left the lot for the shack by the tracks. He said he crossed over the rails to the smoking section of town (the downwind side of the tracks) and made a left on Hatchetbury Road fronting the main line of the Burlington Northern Santa Fe.

Don't ask me why, said Henry, but Hatchetbury Road always reminds me of a gun duel in the days of old and the duels nowadays fought over private property boundaries amid threats with a pig farm. But that is a different story.

Hatchetbury Road stretched home with Henry already in conversation with Franklin about the dark-haired dark-eyed savioress at the check-out counter. He stopped to look for mail at the box stand by the bowling alley and found a couple bills in the box behind windows in envelopes that reminded him how hard he has worked to afford to live in poverty. He pulled away with the post in hand and idled west up the short slope for the last two blocks to the shack. Henry said locomotives idled in wait in his front yard as he pulled to a stop alongside the curb and remembered not to back his front wheel in and exacerbate the small-scale beaver dam built up in the gutter by the tire.

Henry popped the trunk with the key, opened the gate and front doors, and hauled the sacks of food across the cement to watch their contents settle on the table top before he'd let go the bag.

The concrete floor is cracked but clean. *It doesn't cost anything to be clean!* Henry's mother drilled into his adolescence.

When he had the groceries put away, the cottage cheese and bananas eaten, and the conversation with Franklin about the pretty woman far enough along for the time being, Henry said his restless state was bordering on manic so he decided to please his faraway mother and clean house—vacuum it anyway and wear himself down towards a good night's sleep.

Henry cleans the shack with a shopvac. The shopvac sound, he said, transports vacuum man to the tarmac of a busy modern airport where nothing is done without ear plugs—ear plugs that enable a drift into the recesses of one's own mind to observe neurological activity from an objective distance.

Tempered by romantic intensity, Henry is disposed to log his thoughts on love, he said. Here in his own mind on an airport tarmac with a jet engine in his hand Henry can turn an innocent encounter with the opposite sex into a full-scale classical tragedy, but first things first.

Henry said he must tape a piece of paper on the back of the front door that will become a list of the missing and presumed consumed. It is an accounting ledger for everything in the belly of the vacuum. Henry said he needed to attach a new list to the door because he had just cleaned the tank and filter and retrieved the latest victims.

One must be in the proper frame of mind to operate a shopvac when its pipes and portals are clean and its filter fresh, he warned. Shopvac can pull sheetrock off a wall; swallow throw rugs with the biggest of boas; gather a runner like a dog lying down; tip on its face like it takes a leap to linoleum; and turn any human being into a beater bar at the drop of a hose. If the thing had the freedom of a gymnasium floor it would fall over from fright, he promised. Something should be done about it.

You drag the monster around by the muzzle of its trunk, Henry dramatized, and take a look at the tank to curse the moron in charge of castor dolly design for portable suckers (sarcastically speculating a training ground for space engineers), when you turn from the recalcitrant container just in time to witness a down comforter snorted from bed into voracious snout—the rag gasping all the while for an heroic save—but instead you swivel your head behind to catch a glimpse of the karma can from plastic hell pitching head over wheels down the stairs rationing darling little deposits of clouding contents every step of the way while you scramble on its trail in hot pursuit only to reach the pile of itself in pieces on the floor below, on its side whining like a dying elephant. Horror stricken and with no loss of motion, you turn another one-eighty to catch the long snout and snotty coverlet ending their cascade into your shins so you throw up your hands and join in with a floprightdown to take a dirt bag blow and listen and wonder if it is not the Tower of Babble and you are half a bubble off. It is the lucky soul whose life is taken from him in an instant, Henry philosophized.

He gathered up and hoovered on stopping only to record his losses: pocket aspirins, vanilla extract, tube of paint, dish towel, and an unknown from the mirror area. A sound of sucking was the last there was of it.

Henry said he put the vacuum away, showered dirt from his skin and sound from his ears, reminded as he toweled off of the two deadly potentials of living alone: choking on an errant aspiration and the undetected mole. He said he climbed into bed with his imagination flopping him around on the floor like a fish out of water trying to self-inflict a Heimlich maneuver while spreading a lump of flesh in its irregular darkness across a secret spot in his hinterlands. Dying elephants is no lullaby, he languished. Reaching for lip balm, Henry said he sensed trouble getting to sleep and looked to his nightstand for the first station of the clock.

12:34 AM

Did I take my medication today? he asked no one beside him. Henry said he lay his head on the pillow to open the night and reminisced on the day—berserkers at play in epiphanical chaos; the gravel grave of his beret and the snap in spudman's spam of attention; the *shortcut* through the special glaze at the Bar'n Grille to the relativity drive along the Elk River with the moon as mother of all earth's dumbnation; the *go-sign* of a bar crowd cacophony—and said he sighed when the beam of light through sunburned fog shining down on the lost and forgotten in limbo called to his mind the line *lord have mercy on all them today unhappy and stormy as they are.*

Second station of the clock, 1:23 AM

Shapes formed and moved and deformed and disappeared in the darkness of his eyelid interiors, and stream of conscious-ness took a turn for the phantasmagoric to portend a start at the sound of a car crash across the river. A woman wandered delirious on the shoulder of the road. Do you need any help over there? Henry hollered through the damp river air from a far gravel bar. Can you hear me? Do you need any help? We need money! she shouted back in hysterics. She cannot help it; she is a moth: emptiness compelled to fill with flame.

Third station, 2:34 AM

Mayday! Mayday! Flame out! radioed the captain. Emergency sea evacuation procedures, he announced to the passenger cabin. In a flotation device next to the white bird of baptism, Henry sat singing: See them tumbling down, pledging their love to the ground.

Fourth station, 3:45 AM

On cue of an onomatopoeia for the sound of silent liftoff Henry soared in a flying dream on a draft of will and winged over forests and fields of grass, down corridors of students in transit to class, returned to the ground by a thermal equal to liftoff's grace.

Fifth station, 4:56 AM

Heartwarming with a woman at the turning point of morning, her matrix opened: If you want someone to chase you why don't you flirt with a track star, Henry cajoled and continued. I know you want to have children but can't we just have dinner?

Sixth station, 5:43 AM

A kingfisher flew center stream down a river ahead of a festively painted just-married automobile dragging baggage from its bumper. Baggage that celebrated with hops, skips, and jumps all over the road behind the bride and groom. The heart breaks if it does not turn to stone.

Seventh station, 6:54 AM

She knows how about me. I should recognize this elusive aspect smiling and caressing me. A mental euphoria and physical ecstasy rare to dreams and unknown to consciousness leavened Henry with vaporous plumes from scented angels who turned him over for the one of their kind to whose eyes he inquired of the sparkle in the darkness when with reverence and devotion he knelt inexorably into powerfully articulating gates of heaven, received into the unbounded glory of starless oblivion, completely at sea.

CHAPTER SEVEN

Next morning Henry said he was sitting on a stool at the counter in the pastry shop facing B Street out the window when Richie asked what he was up to today.

It started harmless enough, he assured me, moving towards me, gathering my attention. The whole idea came spontaneouslike over buttered bagel and fresh-roasted nearly half decaf, Henry began.

He said he went to get his cup of 70/30 at the pastry shop on the corner of Park and B guiltless of ulterior motive.

It was a day of shine and scattered clouds with the sunlight interrupted on its eight-minute journey to earth by the chrome and the paint and the glass of the automobiles contending for the intersection that created the corner we sat sheltered against, Henry rambled. At the counter, not infrequently one's eyes intercept the altered path of a sun's ray and one's eyes notice his neighbor intact except for a spot between him and the neighbor's eyes where a magnifying glass has burned a hole in the picture. Henry says he has been unable to scientifically account for the color of the hole between him and his neighbor but said he knows from his days of listening to Slamdammit Mondaymentalist Radio that an obvious answer does not preclude a niche for expensive research.

Henry said moments after the thought of grant paperwork brought his daydream to reality, he asked the lads at the counter if anyone knew where the darkhaireddarkeyed lady was living or where she may be working or otherwise might be found. You know the one who has just come back to the asylum ... where does she live? Does anyone know?

Henry said Ron jogged his mind on the mental tread mill and thought he had seen her at a house in town all right. After a committee sorting of who she was exactly, the consensus had her address as local asylum but she may be working in Bidnith.

No shite?! Henry exclaimed, gesturing an apology by reaching for his lips with his left hand. As he swore with exuberance, the sibilance of the swear rocket powered his right arm straight into the upper atmosphere of the pastry shop. Yes!! Next thing, said Henry, he was dropping the elbow, pumping his arm like a marching band leader, strutting triumphantly up the worn fir floor behind occupied stools, thrusting his arm with vigor like it held a black baton throwing reflections from a naked chrome finial sitting on top of the world.

Extraordinary behavior for me, Henry half apologized.

Not getting much more than a few simpers' notice for his miming troubles, Henry said he reseated and confided to himself that this new revelation on the darkhaireddarkeyed one could solve a big persistent problem. The news meant a shot in the arm of adrenaline buoyancy for floating the dream of terminal happiness.

Run with it while you got it, Henry reminded, timing is everything.

Henry gave his weight to the stool and reveled in the almighty genius that brought him out of the shack today, content to let the roiling butterflies celebrate and settle in his empty stomach.

Henry lives for the flight of butterflies.

From behind the counter Richie asked Henry again just what had wound him up and brought him out so early in the morning. Henry said he told Richie he got a call from the Outdoor Store that the *Mom's Best-Accident-Quality Underwear* he ordered several weeks ago had come in.

Henry's answer to Richie's question was not much short of an announcement to the entire pastry shop. Sitting at the counter on Henry's left and apparently stimulated by the underwear news, Ron seemed to spontaneously drop his letter writing and crash into a raucous rendition of air cymbals when Richie took off down the other side of the counter on an enthusiastic march by the beans and machines on the back wall. Richie's spine arched in a curvilinear hyperextension: face up, eyes to the ceiling, swinging the tuba, from way on the right to way on the left, swaying deeply to an inaudible beat, Henry modestly reenacted.

Henry said his own self had again been possessed by the drum major spirit. It shot him onto the balls of his feet, straddling his stool at the counter, raising his arm high into the air, pumping to Richie's soul-marching meter, turning a puckered expression of quiet command from Richie to Ron for a timely crash of cymbals on the one count and back to Richie for pumps on the two three four. While moving his head with a military snap from Ron to Richie, Richie to Ron an idea conceived immaculately, Henry alluded, crossing his heart with an astonished-looking promise.

Henry said he revisited the stool and executed a thorough mastication of buttered bagel before sending it down his gullet as a butterfly perch when he was hit by a stone with decision carved in it—a celebration for the revitalization of downtown business was in order. Somebody had to do it. He would choose the occasion of his trade for underwear as parade day on downtown Main Street. Henry rolled his head and said pointedly:

You never know what is going to happen next.

In the asylum one does not pass up opportunity, he counseled.

There would not be time for advance notice. The organization and rehearsal schedules would be light. As a matter of fact, Henry said he informed himself, the organization and rehearsal schedules were over as quick as they were thought of: done, *finis*.

Life is simple asylum, Henry proverbed, one winter you don't make it to green grass.

Ron had gone back to his odd board game of shuffling papers and moving his coffee around. Henry acknowledged he does not know much about board games but in this game it appears the player has to write where the coffee cup is sitting. Richie had taken to grinding beans.

Henry said his perception paused on the board game sound scored by shattering beans and retrieved full consciousness to turn to the lads and make a motion for noon tomorrow. All agreed; noon tomorrow at the Outdoor Store. No costumes ... street clothes ... no instruments. A silent parade, agreed. Henry said he had a hard time getting to sleep that night thinking on whether or not to wear the tank tops and jockey shorts as outerwear for a uniform visual. Internal personalities engaged the debate and arrived at the affirmative. Henry confirmed the consensus to the lamp above his nightstand as he extinguished the light.

Noon the next day, Henry said, was coming together. The

waitlady's facial contours moved rhythmically to all notions of startled curiosity as Henry ripped open a package of underwear on the spot. A perfect three pair. Henry said he remembered pausing to ponder how one jockey shorts makes a pair and realized it was in there somewhere. Must be the two leg holes, he solaced himself, teensy tiny increments.

Henry asked Richie to try to get into a pair of the shorts. Fair enough, said Henry, our waitlady was looking a little shocky. It may not have been Victoria's Secret but Richie was into the jockeys, his lightweight pale blue cotton pants blousing from under the skivvies.

The three-of-a-kind moved out of the store and on to the sidewalk to poll traffic, Henry continued. We were taking Main Street north to Park Street, down the middle all the way, cross Park Street, and gather on the grass between the cafe and the underpass.

We had hardly captured the marching moment when a patrol car made its left turn off Park on to Main. Henry sagged and said he made an abrupt about-face on the spot and marched backwards with his eyes on the band, pumping his arm with a snap of the wrist at the top of the stroke and a snap of the wrist at the bottom, cymbals crashing and tuba swaying. Steps were high and knees were popping when he heard the voice of authority come from the idling marked car asking if a permit had been issued for this particular parade. Henry said he told the officer this parade was really nothing in particular and waited for the officer's expression to coin before he gestured a halt by a nod of his head to the high-stepping members. The band stopped its forward progress and marched in place, closing ranks. On a second nod and a snap of his pumping arm to his side Henry said he and Ron quit their march in perfect unison but Richie did not stop.

We tried, promised Henry. Ron and I would check him for a full measure then pick up on the one and go for another two measures and snap to a halt to check him again. We could not leave Richie hanging; he could not stop. Richie was in the zone.

The cop was patient. Mrs. Richie came on a sprint from the sidewalk outside the Bar'n Grille and was able to bring Richie around, Henry sighed in relief. Part of being in the zone is not being aware to get out of it, he reassured.

The officer asked if the paraders could not use a ride somewhere. It was agreed that a lift to the pastry shop would fit into everyone's schedule at that particular time. When the door of the squad car closed behind Mrs. Richie and all were loaded up Henry said he asked the patrolman if he would leave on the flashing lights. The patrolman did not answer.

Heading east on Park Street the squad car passed the natural history museum, and reflected in the storefront glass set off by agitating flashes of red and blue strobes Henry said he saw the faces of success, even if we didn't make it to the green grass of the underpass, he added in admission.

The squad car rolled up to the corner of Park and B, stopping tangent to the curve, Henry described, a solemn sober peculiar stop at the corner door of the pastry shop. The officer faced straight ahead and looked to be offering a deal to the hood ornament, said Henry: If you people will go inside and those of you in the underwear will get out of the underwear I will forget about the permit violation and we can all go on about our day, Henry quoted. Catch and release. All agreed.

Henry said he got out of the underwear and settled on a stool like the rest of the band members as Mrs. Richie went around the counter and looked him in the eyes for a

70/30. Henry said flashing red and blue holes burned into the picture of Mrs. Richie's forehead accompanied his nod in the affirmative. He said he thanked Mrs. Richie and looked down the counter to share smiles with the band and quietly congratulated himself. As he got off the stool to retrieve the underwear he had nervously dropped on the floor Richie fessed up that yesterday he had gotten the 70/30 mixture of decaf to caf confused. I accidentally made it seventy percent caffeine and thirty percent decaf, Richie lipped through a laugh as he looked over at Henry hunkered down on his haunches.

CHAPTER EIGHT

Henry broke the night's fasting and over marinated elk steaks with sliced peaches he said he further committed himself to producing a top quality line of heavy syrup, *Henry's Heavy Syrup*, positively no fruit added. Henry said he just knew his ship was in the mail.

He said he had gotten up that morning with the darkhaireddarkeyed lady heavy on his heart. He recalled at the pastry shop before parade day that Ron remembered seeing her at a house in town. Henry said he was moved to remember Ron had had a temporary job with the census bureau and chances were good if Ron had seen her it was in his assignment area on one of his censing trips (trips in this case being a double entendre, having the old-fashioned sixties meaning as well).

Ron has a prescription for marijuana because severe anxiety medication robs him of an appetite. The pot helps the appetite but it also mimics an erasure on a chalkboard turning Ron's memory to dust.

Ron's assignment area was west of town along the tracks and above on the hill to the north. Henry's shack is along the tracks in the same area. While working his census turf Ron stopped in a couple times to bolster his appetite.

As an aside, Henry said Ron never asked him a census question and Henry did not bring it up. Henry says his personal policy is to not answer any questions he himself would not ask. But more to the point, the counting would come out closer if he were overlooked, he reasoned.

Henry said he was grinning over a swallow of heavy syrup, convincing himself he had seen Ron censing the same area more than once. How fortuitous, Henry thought as his blood quickened. He said he was positive Ron counted some people twice but more important, the repetitions would explain Ron's remembering the darkhaireddarkeyed one— repetitions are good for a dusty memory.

It was probable Ron had seen her and Henry said he swore to flesh out the possibilities.

The stimulating thought of meeting up with the darkhaireddarkeyed one put Henry in a hurry; an unconscious acceleration so natural that naturally Murphy, the lawgiver, took a seat on Henry's shoulders. It made for a difficult time getting out of the shack and on the road.

It started with Henry attempting to cover the leftovers on the breakfast plate with cheap plastic wrap. Henry said he was enlightened to note that getting the wrap off the roll and over a plate of peaches would be an Olympic event of exceptional worthiness.

His habit of dilatory searching (looking for something in the least likely place first) was an especially irksome toil this morning, he said. Once the lighter was located Henry wondered if anyone had ever computed the man hours lost to the genius of safety features. He said he had just asked himself why he has never heard a politician moan about this terrible loss when his ear tuned to Slamdammit Mondaymentalist (SlaMon) Radio to catch his smugness report findings of a new study.

Just shut up! Henry said he embarrassed himself blurting his best voice of tyranny at the radio, Goddammit just shut up! abruptly disciplining himself severely, saying he would never say that in public. His father would be beside himself. Shut-up and peckerhead got the quickest reaction out of his dad that Henry had ever seen up to that moment in his life and maybe since.

Brushing the teeth went all right once he was able to get to it, sighed Henry, but flicking the dental floss off the fingers and into the basket proved to be another handicapped event. He said he is not sure how he finally freed himself of the floss because the last flinging and lashing of the finger caused his eyes to slam shut from the sting of the tip of a bullwhip. When he opened his eyes and cleared his vision he said his fingers were free. That is all he knew, but a gander into the waste bin fathered an imperial nod to the conquered, gloated Henry.

Before he could leave the shack, Henry said he had to break out the shopvac for a quick go at the bonsai wildlife. He had to vacuum up a flock of crows. That is what Henry calls the house flies that die at the window. They hang out in the bonsai clearcut around the juniper stump resting from their trapeze work at the glass before perishing on the sill prior to final aspiration into bonsai crow nirvana. It does not take as long as it is noisy, Henry edified.

He couldn't leave them lying there, he said compassionately.

Henry looked drained and sounded of nasal congestion as he warned me getting out of the house was not over yet. He apologized for the change in timbre of his vocal resonance. It was nothing to worry about, Henry sarcast, someone upwind at the plutonium plant in Hanford, Washington is taking an air hose to the reactor, just cleaning up a bit.

We will all be done soon, he assured me as he went on to say as he was finally getting to the door to look for the darkhaireddarkeyed one he felt something sticking through the sock inside his left shoe. The sock had a kind of strangle hold on the big toe about halfway to the first joint. Henry caved-in that he did not care for the company of his big toe on such an intimate basis for the balance of the day. The hole in the sock with the bulge in the shoe made him feel like he was mostly toe, he explained. It would not do. That would be too much self-awareness for an entire day. Grudgingly Henry said he removed his boot and found a sock of similar color close enough in shade to keep any insecurity about different-colored socks below the threshold of distraction. It was a small but important mental victory.

Small victories are important, Henry added in gratuity, as with age you become a dart board and life sticks it to you. If our man had not taken Sunday off maybe something would have been done about it, he philosophized.

Henry said he needed cash for the expedition from the ATM at the NO SAVINGS NO LOAN if his search for the lady was to be sustained. He said he waited in the drive-up lane behind an S-U-V with the daughter of an S-O-B in the driver's seat on a cell phone to someone somewhere. The W-O-M-A-N intermittently talking to the teller behind the gaping drawer of the drive-up out of the side of a mouth that chewed gum like a twelve-year-old while chiding mom out of the other side of the mouth about baby in the backseat car-seat facing Henry screaming at the top of its lungs. Henry said he knew just how the baby felt.

Everyone wants the answer, Henry said softly to the baby, but no one can be told.

Henry said by the time he got on the road he understood

one profile for rage and reminded himself it could have been worse: he could have been that baby. No matter what, Henry shored himself up—he was committed to enjoying the pursuit of terminal happiness even if it meant keeping the happycamperscarnival at a lengthy long distance.

Henry's is a festival of depression. He will stick with that, he said satisfied.

Henry wheeled away from the drive-up and was whelmed to recall that one must not chain down an eagle in a barnyard. He said he felt the rush of the road through the rims of the fuzztop, butterflies swarming in his belly.

He checked the dash. No lights warning. The gas will do for a getaway. The fuzztop gets better mileage near empty anyway, he gestured with enthusiasm. Are we okay?! Henry asked Franklin, the dog in the backseat. Franklin checked off with curious eyes. Roger. Go with throttle up, ordered Henry.

It has happened to him more than once, he confessed, turning to the major delay story. The bears were at me shorthairs, Henry mimed screaming, dragging himself with his good foot to the edge of the sofa in the shack by the tracks to lay it on me now where he was laid later.

If you are having a moment of heaven, it is a beautiful day, you are warm and your belly is just right. You are on the road in your favorite automobile; no place to go. The window is down ... the breeze ... the smile on the face—you feel so good you do not quite know what to do with yourself. Don't worry, he warranteed, it will go away.

Henry said a highway patrol whizzed by in the opposite direction. He watched the flashing lights come on through the billowing dust in his rearview mirror. The cop took the dip in the grass barrow and whipped around spewing gravel for the chase.

What is he doing out here? How did I get here? Henry begged of himself. I am supposed to be in town.

Compose the blood that it be cool, he conditioned.

As the cop got out of his patrol car and approached the fuzztop from the rear Henry said he wondered out loud where all the noise was coming from and found the cop in the side mirror. There it is, said Henry finding the source. The cop's long shoes sounded like pieces of Masonite siding flopping to the ground, slapping every step of the way.

The cop turned round halfway to my car and started back to his own, said Henry. I got another angle on him, sizing him up, and it looked to me like the patrolman was somewhere around fifty years. He had ... *The Condition.* His butt had flattened out from crawling up his back. It looked to be an early stage of the syndrome, Henry judged.

The officer arrived at my window in his element with pad in hand, observed Henry. He started in as a sensible man with decorous timidity and a decent lack of originality but his pretensions to wit were given away by sarcastic smirking.

Henry said an internal reminder objectively placed his thoughts alongside himself, Franklin, and the fuzztop. The three were not socioeconomically intimidating, he quietly conceded the profile.

Is there a problem officer? Henry opened.

Driving without a seatbelt, the policeman rejoined.

What? questioned Henry, imagining a mighty vision that could cut through a gale of dust and penetrate the mud-obscured glass at white-knuckle cop speed.

You heard me.

I have the lap belt fastened, Henry told the cop. The dog chewed up the shoulder harness when he was a pup.

I don't think you will find that exception in the code book, my friend.

Geeze officer, pled Henry, chuck-a-chum-a-chance why don't you?

CHAPTER NINE

Henry had gone towards the north-side hill in search of the darkhaireddarkeyed one but deep thought had kept him going north and more north and farther north. He was north of the Missouri River in the Breaks. He said he loved the breaks country best but did not know he was going there when he left home that morning.

The Breaks is a place where the natives get lost on their own land. His kind of people, his kind of country: both unconquerable, Henry rejoiced.

It was an all-around impressive big-sky day when the cop bent down to ask Henry for the usual paperwork. Henry remembered the McClelland Ferry crossing but for conversation said he asked the cop what part of the breaks they were in. You are in Blaine County my friend, the cop answered in suspicion. The friend did not sound anymore friendly than it did the first time nor did the look look promising.

Henry said he leaned to the jockeybox, looking in and pausing a moment before looking back to ask the cop if he could help him identify the registration and insurance papers. The cop's nose followed Henry's shoulder to sample the air. Henry said the jockeybox produced a beautiful architectural construction on a map-of-Montana foundation; a field mouse was shacking up in the fuzztop. It was a homey little nest with colorful flecks of graffiti looking like it could have come from parade day on Main Street. A number here, a letter there, randomly distributed as if nature had mixed it herself. One could tell that automobile registrations and proofs of insurance were the makings of a cozy home. Even Franklin came forward to sniff it from the back seat, pulsing his nostrils in appreciation.

The cop was not amused but he appeared to understand the dilemma. He took Henry's license and went back to the patrol car.

Henry had noticed the cop leaning in to sample the air. He said the maneuver made him feel something akin to violation. I was not drinking or smoking. I was driving slow enough straight down my side of the gravel, Henry pointed out. What was it all about?

Henry watched the officer in the rearview mirror. He could almost read his lips calling in the late seventies faded gray Cadillac Sedan DeVille with a frayed fuzzy vinyl roof. He swore he could see trouble in the motion of the officer's mouth.

The cop returned to tell Henry he would have to follow him up the road a ways into Whynot, on Cow Crik, where the judge lived. Whynot? Where the judged lived? Henry quizzed. Chinook is Blaine County Seat but this is an ill wind, he deduced. On the follow, Henry said he could not help but imagine the man in the marked car without his gun, without his black, and without his badge.

I wonder what he looks like licking envelopes when the paper cuts his tongue, Henry fancied. Or in his bathrobe on a cold winter morning taking burger out to thaw, watching it slip out of his numbness and smash a small collection of little bones in his big foot between burger and concrete—hop about the kitchen flapping his wings, squawking like a duck; take a kernel of corn in the heel of his good foot, change his step from the duck to the chicken for fifteen eternal seconds before bending over, squeezing his legs together at the thighs like he was about to experience incontinence; cooing and hissing to the heavens.

Oh! And the uniform looks rather gathered to the proctologist now does it not? Henry rallied.

Yeah, a pretty tough-looking customer, he assured his inventiveness.

Henry said he grew up with the children of longshoremen. Guns were for cowards and money for sissies. Power dressing was for Cock Robins. But that is another story—or is it?

When they competed in sports with the posh schools Henry had watched the kids get out of their fancy clothes and earn whatever they were going to get.

The patrol car came up on Whynot with the fuzztop in tow, coming along through the dust. In shadow of the Bears Paw Mountains the exaggerated concentration the short parade received from a thousand bovine eyes looked to Henry like a second coming of the cow.

Into a smallish room from a side door off a side street of a seemly settlement Henry said he was taken, printed, photographed, and held before the questions came.

When was the last time you crossed the border?

Which border? asked Henry.

The Canadian border, the officer mashed out between his teeth. You want trouble?

Not at all, answered Henry. It has been quite a while since I have been across the Canadian border. I played music at the Stampede a few years ago.

Henry looked out through the dangling drapes to see Franklin witnessing a sheriff's uniform combing the fuzztop. Old as it was the sheriff would find a work permit in the jockeybox if it had survived the nest making.

The cop looked up from his note taking to get Henry's attention by informing him he would be needing an attorney.

An attorney! Henry startled 'round.

I am arranging a hearing on the warrant for your arrest on trespassing charges in Carp County, the cop explained. The judge will be in for the hearing.

Henry had had a trespassing/rancher episode a few years back. The Sheriff did not serve a warrant in the case. Was that it? he wondered.

The closest lawyer is twenty-three miles away in Wherefore, the phone is right there, pointing and gesturing *here* as he handed Henry the number.

The attorney will be over in two hours. That will make it four in the afternoon, Henry said he computed, looking beyond the desk to a shelf clock half hidden by an angel's confirmation photo. Henry worried a weekend in captivity.

Silence held until Henry broke:

Man is a roving animal and has an unalienable right to walk anywhere and everywhere on the face of this earth that nature herself has not put beyond the bounds of human limitation. Trespass laws are intolerable sallies against the sacred, he needled.

Respectable people don't want riffraff fouling up their place. Save your story for someone who cares, captioned the cop, like your attorney, for instance, at the trespass trial.

Henry got the picture. Silence reigned.

He took the time to recall that asylum rumor had an intensified surveillance operation near the Canadian border for smugglers smuggling Native Americans into America as a foil for running prescription drugs. Ah ha! Henry thought he had the answer.

In came the sheriff with goods from the fuzztop. Henry watched as a small kit bag (his ambulance) was placed on the desk in front of him. Henry said he apparently grabbed an unopened bottle of reuptake inhibitors on his way out of the shack and the bottle had found its way to Whynot. There was another full bottle of high blood pressure pills Henry had carried for his uncle on their last music gig up the Boulder River. The sheriff stood the aspirin and ibuprofen bottles from the bag with the others on the desk like suspects in a line-up. The owl and hawk and eagle feathers came from the dash. The artfully napped spear points from a beaded ceremonial pouch. The sheriff untied the black leather satchel that contained Henry's trinity of tools: flashlight, archaeology trowel, and wrist camera. No doubt the sheriff would come across the thousand dollars cash Henry had stashed against the passion for a hot lead to Bidnith.

Henry said he could see a smuggler habeascorpusing before the lens of his imagination.

Mercifully the wait ended. The judge and attorney arrived closing their confabulation in whispers and took their seats without so much as a glance at me, Henry said slighted. The silence broken by a question from his attorney animated Henry to begin to sketch out an answer in an arm-waving fashion. The sheriff cut short the gesticulations, as Gibbon would describe, *by supplying the defect of argument by a plenitude of power*: handcuffs. The court called for order and the proceedings opened. Henry swore of needy men and stratified morals: men of maxed-out credit. Henry was sure they had mad cow.

The cop took over from the sheriff and exhibited the prescription drugs, the Indian paraphernalia, the contents of Henry's pockets, then oddly gothic: the nest. He dug the archaeologist out of the black leather satchel, dropping the point of the trowel on his huge foot, causing him to give up rigid jitterbug moves under a stifled grimace as if successfully dissembling his rage. In perfect folly he doled out the flashlight and wrist camera to the desktop. The folded cash blanketed his pallor with Satan's satisfaction. Henry said he felt prescient.

Mr. McCool can post a seven hundred dollar bond or be held at the Blaine County Courthouse on a trespass warrant from Carp County, Montana, the judge declared. Henry agreed to post bond. The judge asked for attorney fees. Three hundred dollars, the attorney stated for the record.

A convenient thousand, Henry rung up on his register. That gave him what was left of the cash in his pocket from this morning's ATM. Just good enough for gas to get home, Henry urged me through the scene.

Henry Finn McCool is hereby released on seven hundred dollars bond to appear in Blaine County District Court at a date to be set later. Mr. McCool is released on his own recognizance to appear before the District Court of Carp County, Montana, on criminal trespass charges. This court is adjourned. Whack! went the gavel.

When the lights in a room get real loud, Henry covered his ears; it was well past time to get outside. He said his mind was in danger of coming off its hinges.

Rubbing the cuff prints from his wrists Henry tallied up the day on his way out the door. An old trespass warrant, okay, I get it; but what is the charge? There is no charge; not one piece of paper ... not even a seatbelt violation. Will

Blaine County notify Carp County? Henry wondered some more.

Everyone but the patrolman had vanished. Henry turned to see his profile in sunset silhouette shadow on the same seemly settlement he had seen hours before. He said he put his stuff in the fuzztop, secured the nest in the jockeybox and let the dog out for a run. The cop was at the door of his cop car with his hand on the door handle when Franklin, forever the perfect passenger, trotted over, and criticized the cop's left front tire with a lengthy blast.

They took all my money, Henry shrugged a smile.

When you get home find something to put on the credit card and make yourself feel better, the cop counseled.

I don't use credit, Henry engaged the officer's eyes, for diluting disappointments.

CHAPTER TEN

G oing up stairs to bed last night Henry said he fell off his sandal from favoring his disabled foot and twisted his able ankle; causing more pressure to his left side than normal and leaving him stiff in the shanks. He paced the shack to loosen his limp and continued to tell me his story.

With the trespass trial looming day after tomorrow Henry conceded he had had a hard time getting to sleep. It was one of those troubled nights when one gets up to rest and on return one makes the bed for a new beginning, he tossed out.

Henry said every time he looked at the digital clock by the bed to determine the night's progress the numbers would change with his glance as if they were slipping away, escaping or hiding, ducking behind a relative in time. Henry said he decided he would head for mountains on the morrow and hold counsel with Sugarfoot, his mentor in troubled times.

The trial shuttled a sleepless loom while warp and weft struggled to weave a plan. Henry said his short speech to the cop in Whynot kept repeating in his head ... Man is a roving animal and has an unalienable right to walk anywhere and everywhere upon the face of this earth that nature herself has not put beyond the bounds of human limitation. Trespass laws are intolerable sallies against the sacred ... man is a roving animal ... sallies against the sacred ... roving animal ... sallies sacred ... animal ... sacred.

He said he fell fitful and dreamed a checkerboard game, checkerboard travel by rules of the grid with live pawns throwing dice for permits to get on the board, drawing television cards for current grid conditions.

From monumental efforts of walking the lines where black met red—balancing tediously to step around the oncoming— live pawns were sore travelers from checkerboard congestion.

Sallys guarded the board squares, patrolling perimeters for border offenders. Lashing at those who looked to lose it, turning over the exhausted to a playpen of squabbling legalese where one in wait could hear collective recitations of brutalism.

Henry said he listened as Sallys brought themselves to tears with self-inflation.

For those successful of the arduous grid there were government parks every three hundred miles where a weary traveler could rest among huge carnivorous animals confined to the overgrazed. Loudspeakers boomed a radio frequency of detail and death. Shades of coliseums drifted his dream.

Henry was restless. As near as he could tell, he said, the dream began around station of the clock 2:34 AM and it was the turning point of morning, station 4:56 AM, when he was awakened by a cramp in his hamstring from walking the taut narrow line of his dream. He said he went to the water closet to sit half asleep but spasms prohibited. As he stood to walk it off his hamstring hamstrung him and he woke to wide awake.

Henry said he decided to see his attorney, Sam Monk, about trespass.

On his way to Monk's house Henry mulled over criminal trespass. There was nothing criminal about it. Henry had pled not guilty. No bond was posted, no warrant was issued.

He said he spoke with the landowner in agreement: Henry would look over the cows and report any problems.

Over breakfast Monk was cankered with doubts.

All bets were off, Monk said, those times have passed. She'll paint you a scofflaw—ignored your trial and walked about town flaunting a warrant.

What warrant? And my argument! pleaded Henry.

Your argument is irrelevant, Monk shredded. She is going to make an example of you and sentence for criminal trespass is nothing short of draconian.

Henry said he paid a visit to Sugarfoot at the usual time. He started the walk at sundown. The moon came up on a cool clear breathy night and lit the way—up the side slopes of lower Sixmile Crik to the first ridge; drop into the crik and cross to the abandoned road; up the gouge in the hardrock hillside to the short flat where the trail cuts Goldprize Crik; north up Goldprize to the old cabin on the crik in the high-country meadow across the light footbridge.

Sugarfoot is son to the goddess Adrenaline, joy of mortal life. Her gift to him: the length and breadth and depth of mankind. The blood of ancients courses his veins. Only crisis will bring him out of the mountains.

Henry said Sugarfoot always knows he is coming. He was waiting, said Henry, with candles burning over a trestle of red wine and honeyed fresh bread before the walk by moonlight up the southwest shoulder to the summit of Emigrant Peak.

Henry said they dropped off the ridge of the southwest shoulder into the cup of the cirque beneath slides and boulders, took water at the spring, and rested on dense cushions of mossy grass like they had done so many times before the final ascent to the head-clearing air of eleven thousand feet.

Upon arriving at the summit, Henry remembered, he processed a subtle mental knell of premonition confiding to him he would never make another ascent. Henry seemed to suffer a psychological shudder of an undeterminable magnitude at this thought but continued.

He broached to Sugar the trial was pressing irresistibly on a fault line of his mind. And then, Henry said, Sugarfoot began:

Beware when a nation of inheritance and unfinished personalities loses its malicious civility and sly restraint and freezes into permanence the political status quo.

The seats of government have met auction. Gone is government that buffers people from proprietor. Government is the proprietary interest: restless fiend, always alive, ever active.

The seats claim to act on law as if there is no responsibility to its cumulative history. Here the wit of man breaks down. Use your hidden intellect to point incongruities, Sugar demanded.

Wealth's fear is of people with nothing to lose.

It is this fear of people with nothing to lose that competes with wealth's soul of selfishness. This competition of fear and selfishness is what wealth calls compassion. There is no wealth without its scroll of the dead, Sugar added.

Henry said he interrupted and begged Sugarfoot: I have a trespass trial in less than twelve hours. Henry said their eyes locked.

It is a sad time of shame upon this mountain, a sad time of ungrateful immigrants.

Ask of this man who goes forward with charges of criminal walk upon his private earth ... ask him what is the substance of his independence ... what are the ingredients of his rugged individualism?

Ask him if it is not the public who guarantees his low-interest farm loan, who guarantee the low-interest loan on his house. Who guarantees his price supports? Who pays him for fallow ground? Is it not the public treasury that suffers his tax shelters, that suffers his conservation easements? Who is it comes willingly to his assistance in his failures?

Ask him how many times does one pay for an unalienable right?

Something must be done about it.

Henry said it was at this juncture he wondered aloud to Sugar if he would not come down and do this himself, but Sugarfoot went on:

In your noble struggle against muddle and laxity do not look to hand-wringing psalmsingers drawn to the occult by frustration, deifying helplessness.

The sublime beauty of mankind is its willful self-destruction. The time of forbearance has passed. Shake the awe of fundamental fatalism and lift dull minds *til avid eyes glitter*. But don't overheat your rhetoric, Sugar schooled.

Henry hesitated a stride, smiled resting on his right leg, and recalled a pregnant silence with Sugarfoot as they themselves shared a grin, and he continued.

Sugarfoot said he would stay in the mountains for now. There are many more like himself, he said.

Henry heard a vow:

When the time comes we are required, we will move at once, as one, as animals respond to elemental conditions, and descend unnoticed into ranks of ordinary people and take up the cause.

Henry said he left Sugarfoot at the log cabin on Goldprize Crik late that night with assurance he was on his own in court tomorrow.

Judge Seller took the bench with an entertaining blind besottedness. The coffee he drank was naturally decapitating. Henry said he could see the judge's averting eyes close ranks behind a conspiracy. What could it be?

The nicest thing that can be said about the county prosecutor is that Chastity NoLie just doesn't get it; Henry stalled his step for an astonished indulgence. She wants a television reputation. She is in it for the climb. Although at the time Chastity was new to the asylum, she belonged; Henry gestured open arms. Folks first thought of her as their local Godiva after her habit of riding horseback in birthday attire. There was no judgment, no clue to the clinging climber she wanted to be.

However, said Henry, Lovingtown learned she was out to make her indelible mark.

In his youth Henry excelled as an athlete. It would be NoLie's triumph to cripple him.

With principal courtroom personnel assembled, Henry and Monk made four. Henry was reminded of Sugar's adage: Two is company, three is a crowd, and four makes a religion. There was bound to be a sacrifice, Henry swallowed.

To favor authenticity by pretense of antiquity, Henry was gathered for solemn oath. He could have sworn he glimpsed the darkhaireddarkeyed lady duck behind the door to the courtroom at the catch of his glance but he swore to god she caught his eyes. Everyone is asked to swear to god except the people in the courtroom who know most about the law.

Chastity made her case.

It was all true, Henry said he confirmed to the judge, it

just didn't happen like that. I admitted to trespass...I pled not guilty with an explanation, Henry's eyes glistened.

Mr. McCool—Henry brought the moment forward—there is nothing you can say that will in any way affect the decision of this court.

Man is a roving animal ...

Mr. McCool!!! Please!

... trespass laws are intolerable sallies ...

Mr. McCool!!! I am warning you!!!

... to walk is an unalienable right ...

Bailiff! Remove the defendant from the courtroom at once.

... How many times do we have to pay ... ?

The knell of guilt was tolled, said Henry, and the cell door slammed. He looked back. There is always a knife on the Ides of March, he reminded.

Henry ceased his hobbled pacing and seated himself in a chair at the central table in the shack. He took a deep sigh and recited from transcript the sentence meted out in his absence:

This court finds for the prosecution. The defendant, Henry Finn McCool, is found guilty of criminal trespass. To appease the offended and expiate the crime, sentencing guidelines require disabling an Achilles tendon as prescribed by law for conviction on criminal trespass. Disabling shall be accomplished by force applied to the longitudinal axis of the tendon until severance.

The retelling disfigured Henry's face. He rocked back in the chair and stared through the transcripts, through the table, to god knows where. Moral and physical revulsion robbed him of his capacity for full expression. There was extended silence before restart.

Henry lowered the chair's front legs to the floor and braced himself:

The severance procedure is to be carried out under influence of paralyzing chemicals without benefit of anesthesia or pain medication. The procedure is to be followed by a series of psychiatric evaluations to determine whether an adequate level of trauma has been administered.

In five years Mr. McCool is eligible for tendon repair in accordance with good behavior under the aforementioned sentencing guidelines.

Sentence shall be carried out at Calvary Hospital, Bidnith, Montana. May god have mercy.

So strive the figures on our mortal stage, Henry quoted under his breath from his reading.

Henry broke it off to let it rest but recalled for me Sugar's last words upon taking his leave in the mountains:

Henry, Sugarfoot encouraged, don't worry, remember: the wind blows and then it storms: that is the way it is.

·

CHAPTER ELEVEN

Prior to his trial one of the deputies overheard Henry talking about flying dreams. Henry told of learning to interpret gravity psychologically by psychologically interrupting gravity with flying dreams. Flying was over the top. Upon Henry's conviction the judge decided not to take any chances ignoring the metaphoric and ordered Henry held in the Carp County Jail as a flight risk.

With pleases and thank yous, bananas and heavy syrup made the menu of Henry's last meal before cuffing, loading, and transportation to sentence execution. Destination: Bidnith.

Henry said he was taken to Bidnith in the back of a windowless van under damp, low, overcast skies. He said he faced the rear doors in the far back and thought to occupy his mind.

To avoid an impulse of noble despair Henry said he decided to recite passages from literature as a basis for determining transit time to Bidnith.

He said he also wanted to get a feel for direction so he switched on an internal global positioning system and computed the grades, bumps, twists and turns along the road to Calvary Hospital, logging them in his mind—multitasking with recitation and time.

For his first recital, he said he turned to a monologue written by Sugarfoot and let on he forever enjoyed escaping within it.

The van pulled out and Henry got his systems underway:

Once upon a life they called me Bear With Sugarfoot, a white paw on the left hind she said she saw.

... the van crossed a gutter and made a right ...

I remember this country. I remember here a quiet river valley. I remember my native peoples and plains aplenty with native animals. I remember the time when with little warning colorless but encouraged people came streaming into my mornings as if rays of a rising sun. Sunset offered no relief.

... a block or so ... a stop ... and a left turn ...

Though Bear With Sugarfoot knew it was his own breath that burned him to death, this time in his later years he would die of capture in a dream of the chase. Dead in his sleep of adrenaline.

So I had thus been born again to my father, my son, a trapper on the waters of the Abzorkees. The mother of this nature would restore to me when she would smile and call. She played my feet and nibbled my toes and smiled and called to me. Sugar was my nickname from her. I cannot tell you who I really was, you would not believe me.

She played my feet then I played the west river in the bouldered valley until the great commotion. People, places, and things seemed to be coming out of nowhere. Cattle were driven, sod rolled from the plow, ore was taken, and independence was shaking. Forests were cut down not burned and me in déjà vu. The West Boulder River choked up so thick with rail ties you could cross it anywhere on foot so I followed my dreams and those ties down to the Elk River and decided from there my best chance would be against the current.

... van stopped and idled at what must have been a traffic light ...

I remember that rail bed being laid, heading west with the sun to the big bend, looking up from the river, seeing those men working in pairs, driving home the rail spikes into the ties lying there in a ballast of gravel covering the once-undisturbed earth. The peaceful wilderness silence broken by grunt and groan, the ring of hammer upon spike, and me pulling water to the back of my canoe as I made my way up river.

... van rolled again. Henry marked ...

Having trapped for a living on the upper Elk during the time that rail was going in and having seen it finished I decided it was high time for some real adventure.

So early one cold morning in 1889 I believe it was, I pulled into what was once a work camp, Quirk City, but now was the town of Lovingtown, Montana Territory. Progress was changing things again.

... van crossed one set of tracks, we must be headed west. Henry was convinced ...

I landed, pulled up, sold my traps, mule, panniers, boat, and all and got myself a job on the Northern Pacific.

I worked my way up the ladder from ball-bearing massager to fireman through the turn of the century from brakeman to conductor to engineer. Then I got off the road and into repair, from the roundhouse to the backshops where I was a union agent until I jumped track to management. I could see it coming. The busymen could see I could see and my labors were rewarded with penultimate promotion to Chief Executive Officer of the Burlington Northern. I had made it to the top by seeing to it that during the merger of the early seventies all the right promises were made. However, when the busymen finally dumped the line in nineteen and eighty-five I had moved on from the traces of corporate harness.

Fortunately (thanks to those people with respect for their own history and admiration for the quickly spent traditions of a free people) all has not been lost or forgotten.

... van braked for a sweeping, fairly tight left turn ...

As for me, I change my shape and come back and celebrate whenever I get an invitation. My present tense being so well described in the immortal words of Lyndon Johnson, a boyfriend of mine when I was a girl in Texas. Lyndon said, he said, Harlot, love, never pass up a free meal or a chance to go to the men's room.

... van made a near stop and strained a hard right to pull a grade accelerating ...

Henry said there were many more motions and recitations but he cut to the chase where he was escorted in a hurry from van to gurney. As he was uncuffed and strapped down Henry said he could see an image developing on the photo paper of his mind of his glance from Calvary Hospital to the gilded ghetto below.

Beldame, an ugly old nurse, appeared gurneyside with her Furies to carry out orders without question. The Nurse Ratchet type chewed ruminatively over a smile of loving malevolence. Out of the glare Nurse Beldame quizzed Mr. McCool with questions she knew the answers to and left the room. Strapped to the gurney, Henry said he gathered calm by closing his eyes and recalling two of his favorite literary paragraphs from *At Swim Two Birds*, reciting them not quite under his breath:

Tuesday had come down through Dundrum and Foster Avenue brine fresh from sea travel. A corn-yellow sun drench that called forth the bees at an incustomary hour to their day of bumbling. Small house flies

performed brightly in the embrasure of the window. Whirling without
fear on imaginary trapezes in the limelight of the sunslants.

Dermot Trellis neither slept nor woke but lay there in his bed, a
twilight in his eyes. His hands he rested emptily at his thighs. His legs
stretched loose-jointed and heavily to the bed bottom. His diaphragm,
a metronome of quilts, heaved softly and relaxed in the beat of his
breathing. Generally speaking he was at peace.

Pressure for an ultimate performance helped Henry con-
tain his roiling self.

As he was wheeled into the operating room he said he
held on to words of his father:

Come on Clutch, Henry's dad would call to him when he
was at bat in baseball. Hang in there, Clutch, you can do it.
Way to go, Clutch, he would tell Henry after the game, atta
baby. To Henry, his father may as well have been calling him
Mister October.

Hang in there, Clutch, you can do it! Henry said he could
feel his dad give him strength and so sustained himself. I will
find a way; I can do it.

Henry said he was given sodium pentothal for intubation.
As a tube was put in his throat for mechanical ventilation the
intravenous drip of paralyzing chemicals was started. The
sodium pentothal wore off quickly and he said he came to
consciousness in a completely disoriented state, completely
paralyzed. He could not see because his eyelids were shut and
immovable. He said he realized he was lying on his stomach.

The procedure commenced.

Something was attached to my heel and calf muscle to
stretch the tendon, Henry recalled to me. When the tendon
snapped my nervous system was rocked as from a powerful
electrical shock. My brain quaked. The white-hot pain muted
naturally but the paralysis freaked my mind, he revealed. I

could not move any part of my body. It was as if my body did not belong to me. I could get no response from it. From tongue to toe it just lay there uncomprehending of my commands. Something must be done!

Henry said he kept repeating, Come on! Hang in there, Clutch. You can do it, way to go, Clutch. He searched in vain but the paralysis was unspeakably otherworldly.

The initial psychiatric evaluation immediately after the procedure suggested traumatic disorder had been effected. He said he was taken to a recovery room for observation.

The toll of torment on his nervous system left Henry exhausted, he admitted. He fell to sleep.

Henry said he did not know how long he was down before he heard that voice again.

Can you wake up? Are you able to stay awake for a while?

Henry said he opened his eyes onto the most wonderful sight he could ever have hoped to see: staring into his eyes was the darkhaireddarkeyed one.

Without hesitation Henry slammed his eyes shut. I must be hallucinating, he quickly concluded. Nurse Beldame must have fouled up the asylum's medication regime. Henry squeezed his eyes closed and again appealed to literature: *Soothe now the tumult of this mortal heart.*

Her voice came again:

Can you please stay awake for me? Henry, please, we don't have much time.

He opened his eyes and felt his heart and mind swirl in dozy does.

I don't believe my eyes, Henry doubted out loud.

It's me, Henry, I've waited so long to see you, please stay awake my darling, we don't have much time.

Henry gasped, he was struck dumb of the entire world.

I am so sorry, the apparition said leaning in, dark hair coming forward over her cheeks as dark eyes moistened.

I have been looking for you everywhere. Where have you been? Henry craved through pain.

A certain someone has been doing everything she can to keep us apart, Henry. I'll tell all I know but never mind that now, they will be moving you soon. I brought you something for the pain. Here is some water ... take them right away. She looked around to the door and dropped them on his tongue.

Henry said it is hard to swallow when someone's watching, especially lying on your back swallowing pills. The darkhaireddarkeyed one turned her radiance aside for one eternal moment of profile.

I will come to you before you leave Calvary Hospital, she whispered solemn. Are you going to be all right? drifted vaporously from the lips as a diamond condensed at the bottom of the left eye and meandered down her jeweled cheek.

Yes, said Henry, I am going to be all right. All's well? She rounded glistening eyes.

All's well.

CHAPTER TWELVE

Henry reached out his hand upon taking leave of Nurse Beldame: I shall deny myself the pleasure of enjoying your further acquaintance, he said while smiling disingenuously.

The sheriff's van was late arriving for the return trip to Carp County. Henry said he sat in a wheelchair by the exit looking over a broken late-afternoon sky while his attendant was away making a call.

Dhde, the darkhaireddarkeyed one, appeared out of nowhere. She wheeled Henry into a nearby autoclave room, closed the door and handed him a bag of pain pills to hide on his person.

We'll meet midnight tomorrow at the storage units next to my shack, Henry whispered the plan. Leave your car in the middle of the others at the muffler shop and walk down the alley to #33. I'll have it ready. We'll meet in secret this one time for you, darling, and then our love meets the light the day.

Thank you, Henry.

Knock three times, he directed.

Henry said he was released from sheriff's custody surprised to find the fuzztop still parked behind the cop shop. He drove home in spite of his lower left leg bound in plaster positioned to prevent healing of the Achilles tendon.

Henry said he had to laugh at his getting way ahead of himself in love. He had found himself daydreaming over dinner about inviting everyone to the wedding before he even proposed because he worried when he asked the question the whole thing would be off. At least he would have had that much fun, he weakly joked.

Henry said he caught himself nearly finishing the cottage cheese trying to level it off in the container before it went back in the frig but knew for sure his mind was aloft when at the top of the stairs he raised his good foot for a step that was not there, suffering startled embarrassment from the clumsy pawing of a counting horse but thankful to be spared a fall.

Working around the cast to undress for bed Henry discovered a hole in his sock and for the life of him could not remember what it is called when you have to sew up a darn hole in your sock. At least, it was a distraction from his riveting preoccupation with Dhde, the darkhaireddarkeyed one.

It is common for the woman to not know Henry is interested in her. He said it is better that way since all women are good until you pick one. So he carries on affairs in the seclusion of his heart, trying to keep in mind that too much seclusion makes one a stranger to oneself. But this affair is different. Dhde knows Henry, Henry knows Dhde, and it is pleasingly potent.

Henry's eyes traveled the map on the ceiling above the bed as his thoughts chose sides to argue love. For one thing, he said he would miss walking up the stairs in the dark if he were married. A woman won't allow that, he declared. And another thing, you have hung out your laundry for years then she comes along to tell you you don't know how to hang out laundry. You would think it was a wonder the clothes ever dried.

Henry said it is not so much a matter of peace and love but more a matter of peace or love and he is a little troubled by the feeling he would rather have peace than love.

He said he sleeps with his dictionary and when he wants to go round and round about something he looks up a word and then looks up the new word used in the meaning of the old word and then looks up the meaning of the newer word used in the meaning of the new word until the go round comes round to the old word and a ceremonious closing of dictionary and sleepy eyes.

He mulled over the confusing fact he can be lonely at night yet content to be alone in the morning.

The waggle of the woman leads to fetters not freedom, Henry recalled from somewhere.

Henry confided he feels alienated from the rules of romance. He said he is looking for love without the boring strategies of instinctual manipulation: the run and hide chase; the putting on the coat and stalling at the door for a begging to stay; or when she comes on to you saying an old boyfriend is moving to town; or I am told there is someone who wants to ask me out; or I am moving to New York; or simply not replying. Henry said he does not get jealous, he gets rid. Furthermore, he does not chase women. Henry said he thinks he gets the drift of the chase: chase them and everything thereafter is your problem.

Those things go on and on, he said, and swore if a man offered a woman the host of eternal salvation she would say: No thank you, I just brushed my teeth.

Women do not take near the pride in their privates that men do, Henry theorized, and men cannot get that through their thick skulls.

His tolerance for female capriciousness has nearly deserted

him, he also'd on. Getting involved with capriciousness is like going out on the town and drinking too much, spending all that money to make yourself sick.

Oh my god, I'm afraid I am too far down the road, Henry whispered, rolling up on a shoulder to go to sleep. *A body is only good for turning a sleeping soul*, he reminded, and pondered the climax of his latest dreams:

Never before, but occasionally now, he slips from the high wire and falls awake. One will not know heaven without making a few mistakes, he ciphered. There is no need to hurry, you will have just enough time to get to the end of your life, Henry counseled objectively, trying to hang on to the facts of his experience—reality. He rolled to the other shoulder dragging his two-piece plastered tendon reciting Goethe barely above his breath:

And not to live foredoomed, alone, apart,
At last I have to give the devil my heart.

Fresh dreams came to Henry:

By serendipitous mistake he dialed an address out of his phone directory and got someone on the line to ask: When your feet get heavy what does that mean? It is going to freeze solid tonight so get your tomatoes in and bury your carrot, she said. Things are going too good for you, horny devil, said the gypsy, fall in love and go to hell or marry me.

Exclusivity she wants for creating a tension dynamic, tossed Henry. He was put off when every word, every little syllable he saw in her eyes she took as insinuating the goal of her prize. That short unshakable bargain of hers: take over my problems and I'll cover you. The goddamned media has destroyed romance, he snorted almost to waking.

What is all this psycho-pompous BS about age? tumbled

from his lips in mumble. What is difficult about women Henry said he finds in all ages.

Would you rather be a young man's slave or an old man's sweetheart? the dream recital continued. Marry an old man and with luck become a young widow.

The old divorcee, was she not charming but a bit round the bend like? Could she not take a compliment without getting herself up a pole at a right smart spanking pace she would.

Dream words evolved to a deafening love. The darkhaired-darkeyed beauty silenced Henry with an affectionate reproach. They danced the swing. You asshole, she whispered through a smile on the first pass. You bastard, she said, twirling under his arm on the next, squeezing his hand to her face in play. What the hell is she on about now? Henry dreamt.

He twirled round to face a tattooed angel fumbling for the diaphragm that keeps her from the advanced state of sexuality. She carried a sign saying *there is no little enemy*. She is one who seems to have found the distress that embitters all happiness. If I cannot help I will hinder, she scowled. For offenses against chastity she decided on suicide, flinging herself out a basement window.

Henry leapt awake attempting to save her.

In the afternoon he called job service for help with a futon and other fine furnishings for #33. He scuffed around in his cast overseeing the move under guise of storage and cashed out the lads. He shook gravel out the cast and slapped dirt away with dust to become a room off an alley behind an overhead door, dragging furniture and leg, hanging framed canvases, arranging and rearranging well into the night until a soft grotto for a holy grail came into itself on a Persian rug shimmering by midnight candleflame.

The knock came. Henry admitted he tried to maintain a composure of prudence to conceal the terror with which he was filled until the magic moment of witness when it was himself he said he saw in Dhde: the meek inquiry all atremble, the fix in her changeable eye, the nervous smile and restive movements of her hands, the apprehensive expression of anxious lips.

The fervor of the yielding mood had come upon them. Yield to passion though yielding be unwise, Henry purred into her loins. He longed to live inside her and never leave the threshold of her womb. Before the transfixer, throbbing excitement seemed to void the I in converging intuitions.

I can't stand to be without you another moment, she sighed in an ecstasy of fire, coming to Henry fully self-abandoned, fairly gasping for breath.

They lay given over in common union. Love hung suspended in a splendid oblivion outside the limits of language until calming hearts and whimpers of intimacy stitched a consoling comforter of soft limbs and feathered souls.

This one has not lost the love in her sex, Henry marveled.

I want to live for you forever, my Henry, I never want to die.

Do we not die each night Dhde? I have died a thousand deaths since you went away, he wept.

I was a fool, Henry. I'm so sorry. I was awed and deceived by the money and fame in Bidnith.

Why did you leave? He begged for absolution. I thought I must have driven you back to psychology school for a second degree.

It wasn't you my darling. I went away to give birth in peace. I have a child by Beamer, Henry, but I don't love Beamer, I never loved him: it was all a mistake. I don't love him and I won't love him, so his mother, Mercedes, is doing everything she can to destroy my happiness, and that means you, Henry.

A child for our love, that's great! rejoiced Henry.

Listen to me, darling, said Dhde, she will do anything to keep us apart. Oh Henry, you should have seen the vicious grinding of the words between her teeth: My worst nightmare would be going through that ... that ... McCool for my grandson.

Why, Henry? What is wrong with her? Did something happen? Why doesn't she leave us alone? Dhde sobbed, relaxing the heart muscle.

Nothing is what happened, Dhde, wounded vanity is the reason. She treats me with an open, thorough contempt because a blurring indignation from an internal wound bleeds on in her in silence.

What does that mean, Henry? Tell me straight out. Please. What is happening!?

For trouble, my love, there is only one thing worse than having an affair with a Hollywood wife and that one thing is refusing her.

So that's it, Henry?

That's it, Dhde.

God's will be doom.

CHAPTER THIRTEEN

The morning after their tryst in the storage unit down the alley from the shack, Henry recalled that he followed Dhde to work that day. His first trip to Bidnith as a free man, he quivered.

Dhde was not working at Calvary Hospital that morning, he said, but working her other job at the bookstore in downtown Bidnith. Henry remembered happily that at the asylum it just happened to be a free-range day for dwellers so he would probably not be noticed as absent without leave. He crossed his fingers and recounted his impatience to uncover the mystery of Bidnith.

Henry remembered on the drive over looking at Dhde up ahead and worrying aloud to the fuzztop interior (Franklin stayed home to guard the shack) that sooner or later she would want something he could not give her. Bodn, Dhde's boy, is coming up on three years now, he really is a neat little kid, Henry reveled, and he should have at least one brother or sister. Henry leaned forward on the sofa cushion at his shack by the tracks and shook his head back and forth smiling in satisfied but dubious amazement.

Watching Dhde through the windscreen Henry said he knew she was the end of all desire but worried about his self-inflicted aversion therapy—his habit of immediately checking off romantic notions to unsavory realities. He prayed the aversion therapy could be completely overcome now that he had found her: Dhde, the woman of his dreams.

Juxtaposed to that thought Henry said he couldn't help but think over Mercedes' personal history as he tailed Dhde to Bidnith. Reviewing Mercedes' past, he said, served to refresh his memory on the vicious antagonism Mercedes exercised on Dhde.

Beamer, Mercedes' son, was a rather innocent bystander in the history. He was not a participant in Mercedes' *issues* although by virtue of being the father of Bodn Beamer was a player. Mercedes' vengeance was for his honor, she later claimed.

Beamer was not an angle of the triangle. The triangle formed of Dhde, Mercedes, and Henry was not exactly a love triangle but it was a triangle nevertheless and triangular madness grew geometrically out of proportion to all reason at the drop of one name: Henry F. McCool. Mercedes would shake uncontrollably at the mention.

Henry said he wondered at the time if the extremity of Mercedes' hatred could ever be explained. Mortification was the one thing that could account for the intensity; possibly she was mortified. Mercedes was scornful for being refused, Henry accepted, but was there more? The probabilities piqued Henry's curiosity, he admitted. He treasured a search, and finding this answer and the proof, he declared, would be like finding the super-secret needle in the motherlode of all haystacks. Henry rocked to the sofa pillow behind and bounced right back to the edge of the seat cushion. He was visibly stimulated once again.

The Mercedes/Henry story began back before the time everylittlething became a huge *issue*. During this comparatively innocent period Henry said he concluded that the secret to happiness was shedding one's demons. He said he made up his mind that if he was not psychologically developed enough to simply morph into the demonless life of true happiness he would find truth by sifting through what true happiness most certainly was not. Word at the asylum had it that Slamdammit Mondaymentalism had cornered the market on unhappiness. Furthermore, word had it that Bidnith was a thriving hotbed of Slamdammit Mondaymentalists. Henry had no choice. He had to do it. He was compelled to investigate. He had been impatient to get down to Bidnith for close examination of the lay of the land and the Mondaymentalists were there too! He said he was psychologically double-buoyed realizing the prospects.

Upon this adrenalin gift from the almighty, Henry said he swore to promptly take leave of the asylum's relatively Rosicrucian Society and go forth into heathen lands and bring back the statement on Slamdammit Mondaymentalists. As fate would have it, the first Mondaymentalist he said he came across was Mercedes Kaltwasser introducing herself at his arrival reception in Lovingtown. From the opening salvo of flirtations Henry said he knew he was on notice of her great expectations.

Henry said as he followed Dhde over the pass he shook his head and wondered how such animosity could have come about among once-friendly people. Part of Henry's bafflement was that Mercedes (once a fan of his work) had publicly supported him and would do anything for the cause of Henry's program, *Voices from the Bin*, the radio voice of the asylum. However, the truth of the new Mercedes was revealed while Henry was attempting to expand the listening audience. Mercedes had had a cell phone accident.

It did not seem possible but firsthand evidence put Mercedes square in enemy camp. Henry said he had to believe it: he caught her red-handed and she didn't even know it. She didn't give him the chance to get a word in edgewise.

In keeping with his form of deep concentration Henry furrowed his brow, focused his eyes inward and leaned back to the sofa pillow while relating Mercedes' cell phone accident incident.

He had just spoken with Mercedes on the phone, he began. She wanted to know how progress was coming along at KPUT SlaMon Radio for broadcasting *Voices*. She told Henry he could count on her for help even if only for reference, should he need to convince anyone of the powerful prestigious support that was behind him and the *Voices* program for enlarging the broadcast audience. The reassurance was reassuring and welcome, Henry came across forthright.

Then Henry said he got another call, back-to-back phone calls in fact, and said he answered the second without the usual hello with the little pitch hike at the end for pleasantry's sake because his mind had wandered in concentration on the first call. Another cell-phone caller? He recalled questioning himself with hope of collecting presence.

Listen Mister Station Manager, Henry said he heard on the heels of his hello, I am calling you right back to let you know I just talked to McCool and he still thinks there is hope of being broadcast on your cute little station, Mister Manager. The woman's voice then proceeded to deliver a clinched teeth ultimatum: If I hear McCool's voice coming out of your precious little fiefdom Mister Station Manager you can kiss your sweet phony ass goodbye, and by the way Mister Manager, if leaving McCool to believe he has a chance of being broadcast is some sick joke of yours end the joke and end it now! I want deep disappointment for McCool, Mister Manager, and I want deep disappointment now! Do you understand me, Mister Manager?! Now!!! If you want to lose your cozy little home with your cozy little loving wife and thousands for your little fund drive Mister Station Manager you just go ahead and put McCool on the air and try me!

Henry said he was confused for only a moment before he recognized Mercedes' voice and realized she thought she was talking to someone else. Why should I tell her? Henry asked rhetorically. Moot point, he said he pointed out to his mind at the time, she has hung up. In more ways than one he pardoned his pun and smiled at his alliteration and rhyme.

It did not take Henry long to figure out that the lovely sweet Mercedes, in the throes of fit, must have hit the redial button thinking she was getting right back to Mister Station Manager. An awful pity but convenient for Henry, he sighed. It had moved along the radio broadcast mystery a quantum leap from where the mystery stood before the cell phone accident incident.

Money and blackmail? He queried himself. How utterly unimaginative, his judgment passed. He said disappointedly he had held out hope there would be more to the broadcast problem than the standard run-of-the-mill stuff. It is a very small cage that predators roam, he noted.

Background info forced to the fore by happenstance, he recalled the enlightenment—good timing.

Henry admitted constantly committing and recommitting himself to stay with the KPUT SlaMon Radio investigation for a full and complete explanation of the negative turn of events, all the while conscious he must be fully prepared to leave on a moment's notice and make haste to the asylum should the time come. What a relief it was with Dhde up ahead, said Henry. The thought of her alone floated his emotions.

CHAPTER FOURTEEN

Mercedes' redial accident on the cell phone cut the puzzle of KPUT SlaMon Radio mercifully short but Henry said the curtain had begun to draw back on the drama shortly after he met with the station manager a few years ago. Henry said he was given the go-ahead to send in recordings and the station would broadcast *Voices from the Bin*.

Henry got home and fired off a half dozen episodes of *Voices* through the post along with a letter asking for broadcast date confirmation. He waited for a response: an acknowledgment of receipt. He said he found himself waiting for anything and waited some more. He said he posted another letter and waited to hear back. He waited and waited and waited some more. The station manager was a busy man, he said he reassured himself, but how busy could he be?

Remember Henry had set his internal clock ticking when he left Lovingtown behind Dhde on the drive over to Bidnith. The trip was going to come to a close fairly soon, Henry surmised. He said he had set his internal clock as a time frame for this trip, referencing the trip to Calvary Hospital when his trespass sentence was carried out. By internal clock referencing he had ten minutes to Bidnith.

Dhde was so beautifully reassuring up ahead through the windscreen that swarms of butterflies were making touch-and-go landings in the belly of his beast.

For the last of that first drive to Bidnith Henry said he pulled up from his memory-file and projected onto the interior screen of his forehead Longtimer dramatically staging the questions most asked by Bidnith people: what is the father like? (arms spread to the heavens) what is the son like? (shoulders shrugged) and whose ghost is it in the ghosthouse? (both hands holding his head at the temples) were the answers in traffic flow? (finger drawing on palm) pedestrian malls? (fingers walking on the back of hand) or was it in downtown beautification? (a righthand arm-wave scribing an unknowable arching path).

More curious yet, Henry guaranteed me, believe it or not, for Slamdammit Mondaymentalists the cemetery is the big mystery. For some reason the Slamdammit Mondaymentalists just cannot get death through their thick skulls, it is said.

In Bidnith there is only one true cemetery. The many false cemeteries, he added, are said to be where non-believers have buried dried cabbage against the day of holocaust.

At least that is how that part of the story came down to him from a deep-ended Slamdammit Mondaymentalist infidel at the asylum who asked that his name not be used, Henry said, adding he was about to enter the City of Bidnith and find out for himself.

Dhde turned off the interstate and approached Bidnith from the east. Henry checked his internal clock ... less than two minutes to go. He said he was half a block behind Dhde when he came to the city limit and read the sign: *Welcome to Bidnith*, and the scripture beneath, *Live in Turmoil—Die in Peace.*

He followed Dhde into Bidnith for his first free time, located the bookstore where she worked on his mental map, and got giddy from getting to Bidnith.

Henry said he drove past Dhde in her parked car, waved himself off, and went back to the east edge of Bidnith and parked parallel on Main to organize a proper plan of investigation: begin the beginning. He said he got out the map of Bidnith Dhde had given him that morning and began a yellow highlighting of cemetery locations when he was interrupted by the sound of car doors slamming. Henry said he looked up from the map to notice, just off to his right in a parking lot, Station Manager and Young Female Radio Personality move away from their cars like pair's synchronized swimming competitors. He said he pulled up the map to cover his face and peered out over the edge. They must be having a SlaMon Radio seminar in Bidnith, he noted. It did not look to Henry much like a convention-type hotel on the edge of a city's limit but that did not mean it wasn't. After making a note of the incident in his frontal lobe log under Merce/StaMan/Yng-FmRaPer for matching up puzzle parts at the end of the day, Henry said he shamed himself and went back to highlighting the cemeteries on the map with his yellow highlighter.

The door-slamming interruption caused Henry to lose his concentration for cemetery locating. He said he paused his highlighting once again to go through the cemetery investigation checklist. This checklist procedure had become much like a nervous tick when his anxiety for action reached a certain threshold of agitation: fresh batteries in the flashlight, wrist camera powered up, archaeologist's trowel under the fuzztop's front seat in the black leather satchel. The cops took his money but that did not matter, the investigation was rolling at its own expense.

Henry said the sighting of Station Manager in the motel parking lot sent his thinking off on another ramble over the KPUT SlaMon Radio fiasco.

He said he will not argue against the fact that most of what goes on in the asylum is better left in the asylum but there is a lot of talent cooped up in the loonies cooped up in the bin and he thinks most of the outside world is missing an enrichment in their lives that dwellers provide.

Since 1979, Henry said he has organized an outlet for the performance talent at the asylum so the talent would not go completely unutilized. The *Voices from the Bin* program has been heard on radio ever since.

We are all found of our animal matter, Henry quoted Joyce under his breath.

Henry said he sat in the fuzztop on East Main Street in Bidnith watching the pair's synchronized swimming competitors walk towards the motel and considered Mercedes' position over Station Manager explained.

The cell phone redial accident incident set Henry straight on the politics of the broadcast problem, he repeated. He said he knew now why it was not going anywhere. Mercedes' threat gave Station Manager good reason to examine *Voices* from an altogether jaundiced point of view.

Henry said the only way he could deal with the politics of SlaMon radio and hope to cope was to write the experience down. Get it out of his mind and onto the paper. Let the paper worry about it.

Henry got up from the sofa cushion and went to a file cabinet and produced his first KPUT notes written on the margins of the Bidnith map at the moment of the synchronized swimming routine:

Station Manager -dash Midwestern immigrant. Recent Midwestern Immigrants /slash like flies that land on swatter -dash squat swatter for speech platform -dash impress upon less-qualified proper sense /slash inferiority. Station Manager -dash confident support /slash important constituencies -dash max important /slash Slamdammit Law. Station manager -dash sure safe /slash Mercedes -dash Slamdammit protector.

Henry said his first notes ended there.

Looking for a reason to be optimistic he said he braced himself for more of the Bidnith/Slamdammit investigation with the two things he had going for him: access and time. On the first count, Bidnith is open seven days a week and proud of it: plenty of access; on the second count, Henry thought he could easily make weekend sorties from the asylum with Dhde's help and asylum weekends are everything from Wednesday on: that is plenty of time. All he really had, Henry remembered chuckling to himself, was time ... and the winds of destiny. It was going to get done.

Chapter Fifteen

After arriving Bidnith and seeing Dhde to work at the bookstore that first trip over, Henry reminded me he had parked on Main Street to locate cemeteries on the Bidnith map but was interrupted by a door-slamming introduction to the pair's synchronized swimming competitors. With his concentration shattered and scattered he said he went to a coffee shop to map out a route for visiting the various graveyards he had highlighted in yellow on the map.

He said his mind was still rapt by the pair's swimming featuring Station Manager and Young Female Radio Personality so without deliberate thought, he said he picked up a newspaper and found himself scanning the ads and headlines for a SlaMon Radio Seminar. He said he did not find a seminar in the newspaper, at least not that newspaper. There must be other papers besides the *Comical* in Bidnith. It is probably in one of the other Bidnith papers, he decided for the benefit of the doubt.

Stories of the day in the *Bidnith Comical* reported unbridled will and moral degradation in God's Country.

Power Offset by Intrigue, Noise and Smoke, All Is Fair in Love and Bidnith, Tragic Topsy Turvydom were headlines, Henry recalled, nothing out of the ordinary for the times.

For no particular reason as Henry seemed to pause to

ponder fate, an article caught his attention, he said catching himself. The headline read: *Developers Finding Laws Profitable to Break.* The article went on to say The Slamdammit Development Corporation won a decision in District Court to destroy eleven-thousand-year-old cave paintings found on its land. The developer made a case for the cave paintings being simple primitive locker-room diagrams of hunting strategies and under Slamdammit Law the gavel dropped on a favorable verdict to go ahead and destroy the diagrams for the new Megalomaniaville Subdivision, soon to be Bidnith's new and most prestigious gated community.

On another page of the *Comical* Henry noticed a comic caption with a wicked stepmother living in a vacuum and riding a broom, *pursuing her bustling idleness.* He said it gave him pause for reflection as if it was speaking directly to him. He said he scanned his memory for a medication update.

Henry said he recalled taking a moment of thought review after making his way through the newspaper to conclude Bidnith might be a city of heads buried in television sand.

Hoping a breeze would blow his head clean, Henry said he left the newspaper-coffee shop for the sidewalk outside.

Once through the door Henry said his mind immediately jumped to illusions of Longtimer's Bidnith tales. In Longtimer's story Bidnith was laid out like a cross, he remembered. The story had a father's house at the top of the cross, a son's house at the bottom of the cross, a ghost house on one arm of the cross and on the opposite arm of the cross from the ghost house there was the one true cemetery. However, on first-hand look Henry saw that this part of the story, at least, had its impefections, and in a moment of jogged memory, jotted down in his frontal lobe log to look on the map for a cemetery that was part of a cross.

At a glance from the sidewalk, Henry said, one could see Bidnith was a bustling city of the *parvenu*: short on middle class and long on *nouveau riche*. Henry said he took several snapshots from the wrist camera for a database.

He said he remembers standing on the sidewalk favoring his disabled tendon quoting Gibbon to himself:

In a contiguously smooth society disparity is smoothed out through the middle class. To leave out the ordinary is to transgress against plausibility.

Slamdammit Mondaymentalist Bidnith was, however, a noticeable exercise in laborious opulence and it appeared to Henry its inhabitants were in such a hurry as to betray a deathly fear of certain change. They were giddy from blocking it out of their minds, he surmised.

Henry said he looked at his map, looked up and down Main Street and repeated the action several times to discover the town was laid out one cross after another attached to another. The crosses of Bidnith had gotten out of hand. Henry said the simple story of Bidnith he had been told appeared to be an unperfected fantasy.

Henry said from the sidewalk he found Bidnith to be a garage too small for the automobiles: claustrophobic, with everyone idling television cars at traffic lights, in a hurry, getting nowhere; wearing their best clothes with the look of paint on their faces; talking into the palm of one hand; waiting for a light to change color through the haze with the other. Henry said it seemed to him that no matter which direction Slamdammit Mondaymentalists looked they had to see a man hanging at a cross. He said he did not need a flashlight to see it.

Henry took a deep breath and said these discoveries about Bidnith were enough for his first trip over; they made him want to go home and go to bed. Accompanied by a little vocal buzzing he made a beeline for Hatchetbury Road, Franklin, and the sack. Enough about Bidnith for one day, he declared, and to end this story segment he asked me rhetorically: how did Dhde do it?

Henry recovered from a short daydream of Dhde, I presumed, and picked up by saying on his second trip over to Bidnith, after another long look around, he began researching the Bidnith Boards of Directors Roster on a hunch.

The mysteries start to come together at the board of directors' level, Henry declared. Furthermore, there would be no mystery at all if stockownership was public information, he peeved.

The same people direct from many boards, Henry stipulated with courtroom-attorney-like gesticulations, turning round to face me from his pace away. You don't have to be a rocket scientist to figure it out. It is an easy way to compromise your colleagues and keep *things* under control, Henry staged, waving his eyebrows over a mischievous expression.

Henry said the newspaper article in the *Bidnith Comical* sent him straight for the Slamdammit Development Corporation's public records to find out who its board members were. Sure enough, gold was never mined so easily. Slamdammit Development Corporation Board of Directors: The Honorable Judge Buyer of Bidnith and John Print, Publisher of the *Bidnith Comical*, to mention two.

Henry noticed there was also a Slamdammit Congregational Corporation Board of Directors; many of the same people with two notable additions: Mercedes Kaltwasser and District Attorney for Bidnith, Mr. Oldboy Bargain.

The Slamdammit Development Corporation's Megalomaniaville Subdivision had to have planning board approval and recommendation. Henry said he issued an investigation order to himself, received it, accepted it, and proceeded. He said his research of the Planning Board Commission revealed Mercedes Kaltwasser as Active Commissioner.

No doubt Mercedes of the Slamdammit Congregational Corporation is separated from Judge Buyer of the Slam-dammit Development Corporation as church from state. Henry reenacted the thought out loud with emphasized sibilance. He said a proper study of the minutes for the Megalomaniaville hearing further illuminated Mercedes Kaltwasser as star of the Planning Board Commission in favor of Megalomaniaville approval.

Henry said he went to court documents on the Megalomaniaville trial and dug through the transcripts and exhibits looking most curiously for pre-trial paperwork. Okay! He got excited, dramatizing a light coming on in his mind, the clues are here: first clue, the judge in Bidnith recused himself from the case as soon as it was filed; second clue, a motion for a change of venue was made and not contested; third clue, the change of venue went west instead of the usual east to Lovingtown.

The article in the *Bidnith Comical* did not mention any fancy pre-trial footwork.

Henry said the documents had a taint about them.

Questions! Henry exclaimed to me as if it was all happening brand new on the moment, pacing one of the paths in the shack and following the trail back. Why did Judge Buyer of Bidnith refuse to hear the case in the first place? Why did Judge Seller of Lovingtown not get the case? Where was D.A. OB in the motions? They must have ties to the Cave Painting Property that is why! Henry's fingers snapped.

Henry said a little searching and researching turned up

The Mulberry Bush Corporation as sellers of the original Cave Painting Property to the Slamdammit Development Corporation. The Honorable Judge Seller of Lovingtown was Chairman and CEO of the Mulberry Bush Corporation. D.A. OB set up Mulberry before he was elected. Judge Buyer of Bidnith was a director for Slamdammit Development Corporation. And, of course, Henry reminded me of the real poison as he called his peeve—it is none of the public's business who owns what corporate stock. But, however, nevertheless and in spite of, the whole thing was getting a bit of the bingo bouncy feel by this time, he rejoiced.

The questions of why the Bidnith Court recused himself and why the change of venue went west instead of east had answered themselves. How the fancy footwork escaped mention in the press was a memory dawn: dawn rose on John Print, *Comical* publisher.

He said he went into a connect-the-dots trance right there in the courthouse and began to recite to himself in incomplete sentences of mumbled volume: PlanningBoard/Mercedes dot Megalomaniaville/Approval dot Mulberry/JudgeSeller dot Comical/VictorPrint. The McCool Conviction must be in there somewhere as well, he surmised. Mercedes was on a roll: the Cave Paintings get destroyed in Judge Buyer's and Judge Seller's Megalomaniaville favor. Henry F. McCool is brought up on an old trespass warrant, convicted, and sentenced to satisfy Mercedes' vindictive spirit by avenging her jealous slight. Nothing to be read about the little private matter in any silly old newspaper either, all nice and tidy-like, Henry smiled agreeably as bingo dots were blossoming all over the back pages of his bachelorhood.

However! Henry started up with overcurious excitement, he said he had, at that very moment, realized for the first time that the sentence his conviction carried sent him straight to Dhde on the trauma floor of Calvary Hospital. Henry said he knew somehow someway someday Mercedes Kaltwasser was going to bite herself in the ass and not be able to let go. This may be it! This may explain Mercedes, thought Henry, as *double mortification* raised its ghoulish specter.

So let them destroy themselves in triumph, Henry pontificated, standing for a stretch and a pace, a pause before climax, and leave them Pyrrhic victory.

CHAPTER SIXTEEN

Henry confessed he used the Bidnith trips to investigate more than Slamdammit Monday- mentalism. He said he chose to close in on more answers to the Mercedes/MisterStationManager relationship since she and the Slamdammits were already connected. Henry got more than he expected.

He said he kept looking, digging, and researching boards of directors. He said the dots became a frenzy of connections. He said he was not sure if he was reading any longer or simply seeing dots in his mind. Dots would not stop connecting. Dots dots dots. You must be kidding me!? He said he shouted and was shushed.

Henry froze to dramatize the moment—bingo! bango!! wango!!!—drawing a line in the air. He said he remembered reading very carefully, very slowly with deliberate enunciated clarity and reenacted the same for this record: SlaMon Radio Commission Board of Directors, Mercedes Kaltwasser, Treasurer. Henry said when he finished that briefest of monologues he could not do anything but find a place to sit down and hang his head.

Henry said he had already looked into the Slamdammit Mondaymentalist Congregational Corporation's Board of Directors and in disguise he had private-eyed one of the S.M.

Congregational Corporation's pastoral gatherings. Boring! Henry chimed in exclamation, until he said he saw Mercedes speaking with YoungFemaleRadioPersonality/Pair'sSynchro- nizedSwimmingParticipant. Henry said he later learned the young woman was in a Slamdammit Law Ministry Program to learn to minister to Slamdammit Mondaymentalists. The young KPUT Radio personality had come over from Odor City, east of Lovingtown, looking into a Slamdammit Ministry job opportunity in Bidnith. Henry overheard YoungFemal- eRadioPersonality tell Mercedes she was looking to relocate from Odor City but still keep her broadcast relationship with KPUT SlaMon Radio. Broadcast relationship, how precious, Henry smart-alecked, stopping his pace, smacking his lips as to dramatize a mellifluous humidity ... getting pretty sticky around here.

Henry said he was afraid the radio broadcast mystery was just another tip of just another iceberg and it was just that—one tragic Titanic revelation after another. It is all so pitiable, he mourned, like Slamdammit Mondaymentalists worrying about which way the roll goes on the toilet paper holder while they graduate students with enormous debt and call it student aid. Student debt is student aid? he disgusted. But that is another story—or is it?

Damn the dots would not stop connecting, he said he wea- ried: SlaMonRadio/Mercedes dot MisterStationManager dot YoungFemaleRadioPersonality/Pair'sSwimmingParticipant dot Voices/BroadcastDenial. Henry said it felt pathetically simple but somehow graceful as a thousand dominoes falling one onto the other.

It was all adding up nicely. It all made sense. Henry was acquainted with the fact Mercedes was on the Calvary Hospital Board. She was on the Calvary Board's Mental

Health Committee and had liaison duties with the Lovingtown Asylum. That's how he met her the first time! She used the monthly mental health meetings to check in on Henry's *wellbeing*; and Mercedes, always the perfect Slamdammit Mondaymentalist, not getting anywhere with her advances on Henry and wanting to move Henry along a little quicker with a jolt of jealousy, took her job beyond the call of civic duty and seduced the Asylum's Board Chair. The Board Chair's wife could never understand all the board meetings. There are no secrets in the asylum, Henry said with mild declarative resignation, shaking his head incredulously; she had selectively not understood.

The dots dummy! Connect the dots! Henry said he egged himself up from the slump on the hanging-head chair.

Mercedes dot AsylumBoardChair dot ArrestAtCowCrik.

Mercedes had managed the perfect tit for tat. Was it Asylum Board Chair who put the pinch on Henry for going AWOL to Cow Crik in the Missouri River breaks? What do you think?

Megalomaniaville/Mercedes dot Mulberry/JudgeSeller dot McCoolConviction. It all had to happen. Henry's old trespass warrant was moved up the police priority list. Mercedes had called in a chit for a McCool conviction and Judge Seller had obliged.

A corroborating conclusion from a different angle, Henry said pathetically. No doubt every one of them was on board. Noticing the double entendre, said Henry, helped relieve the reality.

This was no small victory ... more than a teensy tiny increment, he said, making steeple hands like prayer to the ceiling of the shack.

On top of the scramble of connecting dots, Henry said staccato-like with immodest pleasure, he got his second corroborating whiff of double mortification and gave the old clinched-fistaroo-up-the-old-wazoo sign, relishing the thought.

Question! Henry spun round from his excited pacing and pointed to me asking rhetorically: How did Dhde wind up at Calvary Hospital? Mercedes is on the Calvary Hospital Board of Directors ... of course, he answered, I knew that! I have known that! I also know Dhde holds a graduate degree in psychology. For god's sake! Henry exclaimed. Mercedes tucked Dhde away in the Calvary Hospital Burn-Trauma Ward to keep her away from one H.F. McCool ... Moi! Henry pointed himself out, by getting her a job counseling trauma patients. Bingo! Bango!! Bunghole!!!

Henry barely got the last words out of his mouth before the laughing fit set in. Henry said through sobs and tears he would have given anything to watch the news of McCool's criminal-sentence executioner waft over Mercedes' face when she connected the dots of her own undoing. She could not have been a very happy camper, Henry crumpled into the sofa in hysterics. Twisting his face from deep in the sofa cushion, freeing his maw from suffocation, he mauled the words: d o u b l e m o r t i f i c a t i o n. T r i p l e w h i f f : D o n e d e a l.

After Henry regained composure and set himself upright again on the edge of the sofa cushion his thoughts stumbled around for a foothold on where to pick up the tale. Dots! Henry shouted. Connect the dots you fool, urging himself on.

Mercedes dot LibraryBoard dot BookstoreOwner! Henry shouted to a life-size charcoal centaur on the shack wall. Oh my god! Henry held his head in both hands. Mercedes tried to cloister Dhde with a second job in a Bidnith bookstore just to be sure she was completely removed from the reach of one H.F. McCool.

This is getting pitiable, Henry softened. I don't have to look. I am not going to look, he guaranteed. I could not stand it. I know it is all going to be there in black and white under Boards of Directors for this corporation or Boards of Directors for that corporation. He said aside that he would really like to know who owns what stock. Dammit! It has to be done.

All that aside, Henry gestured a wave-off, trying to find a closer for the interview session. All that aside, he repeated himself, to read in the *Bidnith Comical* of ground-breaking ceremonies for the Megalomaniaville Subdivision, the Megalomaniaville Subdivision, he repeated himself again taking a deep breath, Bidnith's new gated community ... the ground-breaking ceremonies ... Henry floundered and went speechless trying to find the words, shaking his head as if to shake them out. There are no words to do it justice, he admitted his struggle; and then lifting his lowered head in smiling amazement, Henry gathered himself up and delivered. The headlines read: *Planning Board All Wet: Developer Takes Bath.* Henry said he was hypmerized by the headlines and full of anxious trepidation over the thought of continuing on with a reading of the article when ever so slowly (in spite of himself) he began o n e s l o w w o r d at a time:

Shortly before noon this morning a track-hoe excavator struck a hot water vein on the old Cave Painting Property releasing a geyser of high-pressure steam and boiling water three hundred feet into the air, drenching subdivision supporters at the Megalomaniaville ground-breaking ceremonies. A radio station manager and a young female radio personality were among the victims.

Covering the story of Megalomaniaville for KPUT SlaMon Radio, the two were among the scalded taken to Calvary Hospital's Burn-Trauma

Center for extensive treatment. A complete list of casualties has not been released by Calvary authorities pending notification of relatives.

Timing is everything.

Henry said he caught himself looking for the name Mercedes in the article. Enough! Enough is enough! I was feeling as pathological as they! Henry raised his voice. At times like that, he disciplined himself, I recall Bill Russell, you know who I mean? Henry asked of me, you know, the great center for the Boston Celtics. I will never forget it, said Henry, he gave an interview one time and I heard him quote somebody saying: *Know your enemies well for they are the ones you become most like.*

And now it is time to leave these people. Leave them to themselves. It is all just just just so much waste! Pathetically human, he let slip out.

Henry promised he would forget them or at least forget about them but he had one short wrap-up sermon left:

Like all good Slamdammit Mondaymentalists at the trough of spirituality, he summed, it was about money and revenge. A policy-caused crisis had now diverted them from their farciality and they will not look back. They don't want to know they were not the exception. Whose freedom was sacrificed?

And he added with dramatic pontification:

Speaking of hot, in the name of freedom there could be no better time to fire the torch of liberty! It has to be done! And there is no time like the present!

CHAPTER SEVENTEEN

C onnecting the dots for conclusions on Slamdammit Mondaymentalism was signal enough for Henry but the dead giveaway it was time for an all-out action for the cause of liberty was the state of *election wisdom*. The national election, said Henry, made it clear to him and Sugarfoot that the general consensus of the electorate had consumerism too far gone to dare rein in. *Election wisdom* had it that the only thing to do was go-for-it as long as it lasts: worship the god of economy no matter the insults to the laws and manners of the country. A tame and obsequious public encouraged it, he condemned. The economy is supposed to grow at all costs? Grow? ... Grow into what? Henry asked Everyman.

When he got home to the dark room and developed the pictures he had taken with his wrist camera from the Main Street Bidnith sidewalk Henry said there were not men and women. He said he noticed right off that for the little difference among the images there was really only one man and one woman at best. It is an army! Henry half shouted, startled at the thought.

There is need of gall and resolution now! Henry said inspirationally as he sat down on the sofa to show Dhde the pictures. *Better lonesome than mixing with the fools of earth,* he quoted somebody, wanting to go deeper into the subject. Dhde felt differently about the subject, however.

Henry, Dhde drew out with an intrepid soft voice, admonishing him first not to take this in the wrong way before snuggling up to him to ask: Why do you seem so cold and callous about people at times? I don't believe you are that way, Henry, but why does it seem like it sometimes? Other people have noticed it, darling, and have brought it up to me too.

D h d e, Henry sounded out slowly, the vocal tone making it clear he would rather not answer a question like that.

Please, Henry, she said silkily, kissing his neck behind the jaw bone, catching his left ear lobe with the corner of her lips.

I know it seems like I'm being cold and callous sometimes, Dhde, and no doubt, sometimes for some people I am being cold and callous. What do you want me to do? Try to explain it away?

Try, insisted Dhde at the top of a sweet nothing in his ear.

D h d e! Henry warned with a guttural emphasis providing the power for her wide-eyed retreat to the sofa pillow. It doesn't matter whether I intend to be cold and callous or not, if cold and callous is the perception there is nothing I can do about it now is there dearsy weirsy, he said, sliding his left hand between the cushion and her center for safety.

Slow down! Mr. HeartofStone (Henry retrieved his hand), so much for the disclaimer but ...

If the way I happen to see a particular situation doesn't get beyond myself ... doesn't communicate ... I accept that.

Give me an example of a situation, darling and don't be hard to follow. Okay, please?

I'm thinking Dhde ... all right, the heart is used as a metaphor for something between two people ...

You mean like l o v e? unfurling her curled tongue, sliding the word out down the growing length, elongating the sound, dramatizing her playfulness.

If you want to call it that ... As a metaphor the heart goes like this for me ...

Like what baby? She begged with her right hand contacting the inseam of his left thigh.

Dhde!? (she yanked back her hand) I'm glad to see you're having fun with all this, missy. Silent stares robbed a further exchange.

Okay, my Henry, please go on.

Give me a chance.

I am giving you one last chance before I ...

Before you what? he demanded as he shifted towards her, miming a coming embrace.

No! Henry. I want to hear this first!

Then control yourself.

Who better control whoseself? Mr. ReadyorNot?

Dammit! Dhde!

Go on my darling, the heart you were saying?

The heart must be intact or it is dead. There can't be any chambers or valves missing or shut off or cut out. Everything must be there up and running or it is done ... a lump ... dead ... a dead lump.

So what does that have to do with ...

In a relationship between two people things are going along fine then one or more of the things are shut off ... pieces cut out ... what happens? Death happens, Dhde. The heart is dead. The relationship is dead.

There has got to be more to it than that, Henry.

There is if y o u will l e t me get t o it, Henry mouthed long and emphatic with a twisting half-growl half-purr, a verbal accompaniment to the stretching of arms and flaring of hands.

Henry!!

He answered her admonishment with a slow retreat, warning her with squinting eyes from a cocked head.

Oh! Henry, how did the pieces get cut out? She feigned fainting with the back of her hand on her forehead.

Henry marked her drama but persevered.

When one or the other of the people decide to cut out part of the relationship that's how. When one or both of them withholds something that once existed between the two people it is over ... dead. What once existed between the two people was made of valves and chambers and blood ... a rhythm and beating ... a pulsing ... and then some part of what existed was stopped ... intellectually excised ... cut out ... heart dead. The heart cannot live like that. Maybe a fake or imaginary heart can go on with parts missing, a blood-starved uncoordinated existence, jerking around spastic-like, but a real heart cannot do that and neither can a real relationship. Neither can love. The eyes, the words, the body language ... you can't trust anything anymore.

So when something stops in a relationship the whole thing stops? I don't think so, Plato.

I do.

You are cold and callous.

So I am.

Henry!?

Dammit Dhde! I am not saying it covers every case but I am positive it covers some.

I am not Dammit Dhde, she mused a pout, pursing her lips.

Hell with it! You asked!

Go on, I'm listening.

My ass!!

Please. Can't you take a little joking?

Yes, as a matter of fact, I am going to take every last tiny morsel of your little joke and right ...

Henry!!

Dammit, Dhde! Why do you ask if you won't let me finish?!

Sorry, darling, I won't interrupt again ...

The heart ...

... but I'm not Dammit Dhde.

... the h e a r t f u n c tions only as a complete organ ... so does a relationship.

So where does that get you?

I'm thinking.

I'm waiting for you, warbling a simple melody.

Then wait no longer you dev ...

No! Henry! Please! No! Dhde rushed. You are stuck aren't you? She giggled, raising her knees to her chest, fending off the weight of Henry's advance. He loomed and lorded over her with deliberate, audible breathing.

Death is a superior condition. Death is superior to a wheelchair of amputated love.

That's awful, Henry!! Truly awful!

When the heart is dead I accept its death, he captured Dhde with his stare. I would rather accept its death and go on loving than to pretend it is alive and stop.

No!! Henry!! No!!!

Yes, Dhde, Henry growled an unstoppable slow motion.

Is that it?! Dhde rushed with excited speed.

T-h-a-t's it. Henry confirmed gentle and slow.

So what about the other person? Her belly bounced out an anxious laugh. What if the other person doesn't see it like that? she bubbled.

I have but one life to live and I am going to live it right...

That's callous and cold!!

I admitted when we started this whole thing, he weighed in, that to the other person it was cold and callous or callous and cold. Whichever way you like it, Dhde, giving his weight to her.

So what about the other person, Henry?! unraveling the last threads of resistance, a rigid tickled fit, anxiety through the roof; knees up, head thrown back: mouth agape. So how does that help the other person?! she triumphed over her emotions with Henry extended over her curled bent body.

I doubt it does but death ... is indifferent.

You're impossible! She hollered to the ceiling.

Okay, I'm impossible, he agreed, tasting her throat on final approach. I love you, Dhde, his teeth caressing her jugular.

I love you, Henry, Dhde freed, barely intelligible in the murmur of an exhale.

Tomorrow we give liberty a purchase.

enry said he and Dhde moved from the sofa to the heavy square oak table in the middle of the shack where he laid out the leaving plan for her.

Dhde asked Henry about the cops knowing the *shortcuts*.

The *shortcut* images change frequently enough; the cops could not possibly know where he was going, he reassured her.

We are going to separate and meet up at the spot. You go down the valley and back in just enough time. If anyone asks any questions, Dhde, just tell them we are going for a short *float*.

Henry said he needed to pay Sugarfoot a visit and left for Emigrant Peak that moment. It had to be done.

Henry and Sugarfoot talked of the wisdom of the electorate and what that wisdom was, that the system was too far gone: plain go-for-it was the wisdom.

What we have seen are only curtain raisers on insane dramas to come, Henry recalled the warning from Sugarfoot.

Consumerism is misfortune for the world. The jib is up. The mainsail set. The sign will be seen; the mountains will be on the move. Departure for you, Henry, and descent into the populace for me, Sugarfoot recited with cool objectivity.

It is time for the tough questions on the records, said Sugar sternly.

Was McCarthyism reasonable?

Was the Cold War nuclear weapons production program reasonable?

Was the biological weapons program reasonable?

Is the record for heavy industry on environmental concerns reasonable?

Is the pollution of land, air, and water from the nuclear, biological, chemical, and petroleum industries reasonable?

What evidence supports trust for inroads into privacy?

No response from Henry, Sugarfoot was off stumping.

He went on:

Economy is the god … consumerism the religion.

A partially dismantled judicial system could go like dominoes at any given moment from the language of Justice Department lawyers. Sugarfoot showed a rare shudder.

A war power's emergency without a war, without an emergency, without an end, Henry lent support.

Screen Seekers are the modern monks—the quiet slain, the anti-social unfabric, divided and conquered, an enemy within.

It was time for departure. Henry and Sugarfoot reviewed understandings. Henry will poll the public on his voyage to the sea. Sugarfoot will stay on the Elk River in Crow Country and slip down into the population once the sign to move out of the mountains is complete.

It is very bad news when an Administration, Supreme Court, and Capitol Hill don't like you to be so free, Sugarfoot sighed for the inevitable. An all-out struggle to clear minds for liberty and preservation: *THIS* … is the big one.

Henry nodded on the time that had come to pass.

Henry said Sugarfoot's parting words were a Gibbon quote from the *Decline and Fall of the Roman Empire*:

The experience of past faults, which may sometimes correct the mature age of an individual, is seldom profitable to the successive generations of mankind.

Henry said he knew what Sugarfoot meant but admitted to Sugar that he, Henry, will still try to pull his long pants off over buckled sandals.

Henry said he and Sugarfoot exchanged chuckles with eye contact knowing they did not have a clue when they could acknowledge each other again. Duty called and with a final nod Henry made his way down the mountain, letting the reality settle into his system and vigorously stir up a flight of butterflies.

What a great feeling, Henry came clean.

He got home and was inside the shack giving last-minute instructions to his brother Victor; bills to pay, plants to water and how the pump action worked on the twelve-gauge shotgun. Henry was leaving his shotgun with Victor. He had decided not to take it on the float.

Henry said he had just filled the magazine with three rounds of #6 duckload when he heard loud teenage exhaust pipes and a bashing sound on the roadside wall of the shack. He turned the gun upright and pumped the action, loading a round into the chamber. He said he was about to explain the safety and ejection mechanisms on the shotgun when he heard another crashing, shattering sound come from the road, and more teenage revving sounds. This time he made a beeline to have a looksee. As he pulled open the door of the shack he saw a pickup truck out front with someone in the back loading a handheld launcher commonly used for trap shooting. The driver of the truck caught sight of Henry and punched it to make his getaway, dumping the person in the pickup bed on the back of his head in the box. Henry said he raised the shotgun and touched off a round at the fleeing pickup, pumped again like he was on a trap range and fired a second round blowing a tire, fairly well pulverizing the left rear panel and tailgate of the truck. The driver stopped the pickup and got out as Henry hobbled to the fuzztop to see what damage had been done. The black and fluorescent orange shards of a clay pigeon were all over the road. Henry said he found orange paint spin-mark designs of plastic residue layered on the fuzztop's faded silver paint and on the metal siding of the shack.

He said he turned to noise from the pickup. The lad in back of the truck could not be seen but could be heard balling. Don't shoot! Don't shoot, mister! He cried through sobs. The frightened teen-aged driver took a couple cautious steps toward Henry and choked out: You just shot the shit out of my dad's truck.

Henry said he chambered the last round.

Pull! he yelled. The clay pigeon launcher flew out of the back of the pickup; Henry blew it across the pavement, banging it into the curb.

Don't shoot! Please mister, don't shoot! was the cry.

A perfect score, Henry said with some assurance.

What about my dad? pled the vandal.

You go straight home and tell your father he should come and pay me a visit, invited Henry. I should be around for an hour or so.

The vandals drove off shredding tire from rim as Henry's brother came up from behind and warned him he was sure he hadn't heard the end of the incident. What the hell did you do that for anyway? Victor asked in earnest.

Almighty somethinorother was writing a piece of poetry, Victor, Henry answered matter-of-fact-like, and we were the characters populating the poem. It had to be done. What is that supposed to mean? probed Victor.

We'll talk about it later, Henry promised. Right now I've got to finish getting ready to leave. Dhde will be by anytime. She leaves and is gone from me until we meet at the vessel.

If you don't mind me asking what is this little float all about? Victor queried.

It is about liberty, Henry made flat unquestionable declaration. Somebody's got to do it.

Aren't you going to miss this place? asked Victor.

What I miss are the people that used to live here. They had a way of life you could live by, not just a way of life you could live with. Unfortunately as a doctor friend of mine once put it:

Those people are gone and they ain't coming back.

I miss them, Henry emphasized.

You may feel differently tomorrow, Victor returned the volley.

Tomorrow is just a dog burying a bone, Henry backhanded.

This is home, Victor reminded as they went inside the shack.

Home is just a place to hang your head, Henry attempted a rally, but let Victor know that he was right. This country will always be home, Henry acknowledged with some emotion. It is wake-up-little-Susie time, Victor, and somebody has to drive the car home, he said analogously.

Victor decided to think on that awhile.

Henry said Dhde came back to the shack for the final pack and she made ready to go. The brother's pickup truck was packed and loaded.

Final finals were given the once over, said Henry.

Dhde will be at the place on the river at the appointed time waiting for him with the rubber raft. Henry will inflate the raft when he gets there. The pickup will be unloaded into the vessel.

Henry said he made a final check of the pickup packing and added the black leather satchel with flashlight, wrist-watch camera, and archaeologist's trowel inside before Dhde drove away. The manuscript in the ambulance had already been stowed. He did not want to draw any attention to himself at the Bar'n Grille.

Henry said he remembered being reminded tying his shoe for the last time in his shack by the tracks to pull himself up by the bootstraps. This would be a difficult job, Henry recalled acknowledging, nearly as difficult as levitation.

Henry pointed out to me as a reminder that with levitation, however, there were options: you could take it or leave it. With liberty there were no such options. Every now and then liberty has to be re-secured, he assured.

Henry said he warned Victor the authorities were alerted to his departure plans and to be extra careful with the plans to meet them for the exchange of Bodn and Franklin. The cops had pulled up behind him on the way in to Hatchetbury Road from Six Mile Crik. Henry said he had noticed them on the road down from Emigrant Peak. Perhaps butterflies had given him away.

When he left the shack for the last time Henry said Victor drove him to the Bar'n Grille with Franklin in the back seat. Henry said he smiled at the site of teenage vandal and scolding dad coming from the opposite direction on Hatchetbury Road, no doubt headed for the shack by the tracks: oblivious to their roles.

Victor parked the fuzztop on Main Street Lovingtown outside the main door of the Bar'n Grille at Henry's direction. Henry said he told the imaginary meter maid out loud but to himself as he got out of the car for the last time that if she had a problem with the fuzztop the keys would be in it. He said he laughed at what the collection of yellow envelopes might look like before she got the picture. He leaned in and told Victor and Franklin he would see them later, after their *walk*.

Henry said he imagined the cops in wait for him to come out of the Bar'n Grille so they could take him in for questioning.

Someone said it was much later before one of them came inside for a look around. They wanted to avoid a possible shotgun incident she said.

The hospital death that Henry had lived through became the life he died into.

Never was a man happier to meet the moment! pumped Henry, taking a seat beneath the special glaze before winging his way across a cathartic ocean for a new kow to tow to.

STORY CONTINUES IN BOOK TWO

www.ingramcontent.com/pod-product-compliance
Lightning Source LLC
Chambersburg PA
CBHW021425200626
46814CB00015B/1484